"Do you own another gun?" asked Mac.

Louisa Cormier looked mildly amused. "No."

"Have you ever fired a gun?"

"Yes, as part of my research. My character Pat Fantome is an ex-police officer with a very good aim. I think it helps to know how it feels to fire a gun. I go to Drietch's Range on Fifty-eighth."

"We'll find it," said Mac. "One more question. Do you have any idea how Lutnikov's blood got on the carpet outside your elevator door?"

"No. I'm really a suspect, aren't I?" She seemed pleased by the possibility.

"Yes," said Mac. "But so are all your neighbors."

Original novels in the CSI series

CSI: Crime Scene Investigation
Double Dealer
Sin City
Cold Burn
Body of Evidence
Grave Matters
Binding Ties

CSI: Miami
Florida Getaway
Heat Wave

CSI:NY™

DEAD OF WINTER

a novel

Stuart M. Kaminsky

**Based on the hit CBS series "CSI: NY"
Produced by CBS Productions, a business unit of
CBS Broadcasting Inc. and
Alliance Atlantis Productions Inc.
Executive Producers: Anthony E. Zuiker,
Andrew Lipsitz, Danny Cannon, Jonathan Littman
Series created by: Anthony E. Zuiker,
Ann Donahue, Carol Mendelsohn**

POCKET BOOKS
New York   London   Toronto   Sydney

An *Original* Publication of POCKET BOOKS

 published by POCKET BOOKS,
a division of Simon & Schuster, Ltd.,
Africa House, 64–78 Kingsway, London WC2B 6AH

ISBN: 1-4165-1105-9

First Pocket Books printing September 2005

10   9   8   7   6   5   4   3   2   1

POCKET BOOKS and colophon are registered
trademarks of Simon & Schuster, Inc.

Cover art by Patrick Kang

Printed and bound in Great Britain

A CIP catalogue record for this book is
available from the British Library.

With thanks to Bruce Whitehead and the Crime Scene Investigation Unit of the Sarasota, Florida, County Sheriff's Office; to Lee Lofland, Denene Lofland, and Dr. D. P. Lyle for their forensic knowledge and willingness to share it with me; and to Hugo Parrilla, retired Detective N.Y.P.D. 24th Squad, for sharing his knowledge of New York City.

Prologue

IT WAS A NIGHT FOR DREAMING.

It was the beginning of February, the coldest time of the year in New York, always the coldest. Don't let them tell you about the storms of January or the surprise downfalls and frigid blasts from Canada that come down sometimes as early as early November and as late as late March.

No, you could count on February being the most unforgiving month of the year. And this one was particularly spiteful.

The temperature teased thermometers at the zero level. The winds played angrily, howling through ghostly empty streets in the five boroughs. The snow fell steadily, relentlessly, siltlike, no good for packing or making snowballs when Saturday morning came in a few hours.

City plows chugged steadily, in convoys and alone, trying to keep pathways open on the streets. The garbage had not been picked up. The plows shoved mounds of snow over dark plastic bags, burying them till something resembling a thaw came so that garbage trucks could make their way through hundreds of miles of slippery streets.

Four in the morning.

Mac Taylor turned to his left in bed. He had an alarm clock but never turned it on. He always awoke within a few minutes of four in the dark morning. For another hour he would put his hands behind his head and look up at the ceiling, watching the light from passing cars, stars, and the moon vibrate on his bedroom ceiling. Tonight there was no traffic, no stars or moon through the snowy sky. He looked up at darkness, reasonably successful at not thinking, knowing he would get up in an hour, hoping that hour would pass soon.

Stella Bonasera had a feverish dream. She had just fallen back to sleep after having gotten up to take two Tylenols and have a glass of microwaved tea. In her dream, the huge bloated body of a woman hovered above a bed like a Thanksgiving Day float. Stella felt it was up to her to keep the body from floating out of an open window nearby, but she couldn't move. She hoped the body was too large to fit through the window. Atop the woman's body sat a cat, a gray cat, looking solemnly at Stella. Then the dream was gone and Stella slept peacefully.

Aiden Burn had fallen asleep at about two in the morning trying to remember the name of her second-year high school math teacher. Mrs. Farley or Farrell or Furlong? She could see the woman's face, remember her voice. In what was a dream, or possibly just a reverie, Aiden heard the voice of that teacher reminding the class for the five hundredth time that it was the little mistakes that brought you the wrong answers. "You might see the big picture, but one small mistake, one careless moment, and everything that follows will be forever wrong." Aiden had remembered that more than anything else from any high school class. She had tried to live by it, but still it haunted her, especially when the wind tickled the windows and a deep chill overcame the hissing radiators.

Danny Messer reached for his glasses and checked the red illuminated numbers on the bedside clock. It was a few minutes after four. He touched his face. He would need to shave when he got up. He would do it in the shower. He would think about it later. He rolled on his left side in search of a comfortable position, found it instantly, and fell into dreamless sleep.

Sheldon Hawkes lay on a cot in his laboratory reading a book about an archaeological find in Israel. There was a photograph of a skull located at the site. The text, by someone whose name he didn't recognize, said that the skull was about three thousand years old and had been damaged by some natural disaster. Hawkes shook his head. The hole in the skull was the result of a blow with a rough-edged rock. It was the only damage to the specimen. No scratches, no bruises. The skull was almost perfectly preserved. If the hole had been caused by nature, there would be other signs of lesser trauma. Hawkes needed the original skull or a good set of photographs. There was no doubt the long-dead man had been killed by a blow from a rock, and, since it was assumed from artifacts discovered near the body that the dead man was royalty, Hawkes was curious about who might have murdered him and why. When he finished the book, he would send an E-mail to the archaeologist. Hawkes kept reading. He had already had the four hours of sleep he needed. He was near the bodies in the drawers. The wind was going wild in the streets. He had a good book. He was content.

Don Flack may have dreamt, but he didn't remember his dreams, which was just as well because the detective had seen much that could cause him nightmares. The alarm would go off at seven, and he would be awake instantly. It had been like that since he was a boy. He hoped it would be like that the rest of his life.

The brothers Marco slept half a city apart. Anthony, in holding on Riker's Island, only floated around the edges of sleep. Jail was not a place for comfortable slumber. Jails at night were a disgusting antisymphony of hacking coughs, snoring, people talking to themselves in their sleep, guards walking. Jails were places where you had to stay just this side of awake so nothing and no one would sneak up on you. Not that Anthony thought someone might be coming for him, but you never knew who you might have slighted or insulted without realizing it. Outside, the name Anthony Marco meant something. Inside, he was just another old, white fool. In the morning he would be back in court. If things went well, the course of the trial would change in his favor. He didn't exactly count on it, but felt it should happen.

Anthony's brother Dario was awake. Insomnia. His wife's snoring. His bad stomach. He got up and went to the bathroom where he sat and read *Entertainment Weekly*. He was nervous. Tonight, close to right now, it was happening. He had made a call five hours ago to change the plan. His daughter had convinced him that it was the best way to go, and since he was thinking along those lines anyway, he made the call. Things could go wrong. When you counted on dumb people, you took a chance, even when the dumb people were loyal. Marco had a theory. Only dumb people could truly be counted on to be loyal. Smart people thought too much, looked out for themselves. Marco knew. He was one of the smart people. Hell with it. He went back to bed and nudged his wife, hoping she would turn to the side and stop snoring. She grunted and turned, but the snoring got louder. He put a pillow over his head and told himself that if he didn't fall asleep in the next four or five minutes he would get up.

Stevie Guista dreamt of water, just water, a broad expanse of water. He knew it was cold and he didn't want to go in, but it looked beautiful and all he wanted to do was keep watching it. Then he had the feeling. Something was coming up behind him. He wanted to turn and look at it. He didn't want to turn and look at it. He wanted to plunge into the water. He was afraid of plunging into the water. He stood frozen at the bank of the lake or whatever it was and wished he could wake up.

Jacob Laudano, damn it, was on a horse again. He knew he was dreaming, but he couldn't wake up and he couldn't get the horse to stop or slow down. He crouched over, hanging on, knowing from the position of the other horses around him that he was going to lose or, worse yet, that he was going to fall. He had been a jockey for eight years and hated every day of every diet, every moment on top of the stupid animals he could barely tolerate. He didn't like them. They didn't like him. He had been a lousy jockey. He was an average thief. If he could wake up, he could get a glass of something, water, rye, something. Then he could go back to sleep. He had gotten to his apartment less than an hour ago. He had done what he had to do. It had been easy. He got his money. So why the hell was he having bad dreams. This dream in particular, putting him on a damned horse, knowing he was going to lose. He made the effort, called out in his sleep, struggled, and burst into darkened wakefulness. The roar of the crowd was the whirling of the wind. The breeze on his legs was from the cold that seeped in through badly insulated windows. The sweat on his forehead wasn't from the exertion of the race but a sense of waking fear. Jacob the Jockey was afraid to go back to sleep.

She had three names, the one she was born with, the one she had taken when she married the hedgehog who had slunk away one night when she was asleep, and the name she used for her job, her professional name, her respectable name.

Helen Grandfield was born at the age of thirty, having put behind her identities as a stripper and lap dancer who had failed to become popular and whose tainted reputation had failed to drive her father into a rage. The old man had simply ignored her. As long as she didn't use the family name, he didn't care. He had other children who didn't try to drive him crazy and he had too much on his mind, like staying alive and away from the law, to worry about one daughter. Then she had changed. Just like that. All of a sudden. Took business courses at Fordham after learning accounting. She had practical value to her father now, and was not only appreciated but listened to. She was content. She slept well. Things were going on tonight. Important things. Things that could mean a great deal for her father, for herself. Deep inside she even considered that if things went as well as planned, she'd find her hedgehog husband and have his throat cut—if possible while she watched. Helen Grandfield slept peacefully.

Ed Taxx and Cliff Collier had not slept. They had not tried to sleep. They were not supposed to sleep. They sat in the hotel room, Ed reading a mystery novel by Jonathan Kellerman, Cliff watching a taped rerun of a hockey game played hours earlier. He had avoided watching the news or ESPN so that he wouldn't know how the game turned out. At the moment, the Rangers were ahead 3-1 at the start of the third period. Cliff worked on a Diet Coke. Ed had a Dr Pepper. Neither man was really tired. Too much on their minds. However, a jolt of caffeine short of coffee or Mountain Dew wouldn't hurt. Taxx looked at his wristwatch. Two hours or so till dawn. He was having trouble concentrating on the book. Cliff had offered to watch the game without sound, but Ed had said he didn't mind. He didn't like hockey, but he knew he could tune it out. Ed adjusted his shoulder holster and lay back with the book on his chest.

The girl's name was Lilly. She was eleven, a little short for her age but not much. Something woke her. She looked over from her bed to her mother who was breathing the way she did when she slept. Lilly was reasonably sure it was the wind that awakened her.

She got out of bed and moved into the living room where she turned on the lamp on the table in the corner. It was there, the dog. It wasn't a bad-looking dog, but it wasn't a beautiful one either. She wondered if she should have painted it brown and gold instead of black and white. It wasn't too late. But she knew she wasn't going to do it. She was tired. She might make a mistake, make it worse. It would have to stay black and white. She hoped he liked it even though it wobbled when it stood. She had made one rear leg too short. Lilly got a glass from the kitchen shelf and the chocolate milk from the refrigerator. She sat with a glass of milk and a chocolate chip cookie and continued to examine the dog. She decided to call him Spark. Or maybe something else.

Lilly finished her cookie and milk, put the empty glass down on the table in front of her, and leaned back. She could see the snow hitting the window, not wanting to get in but simply being lazy. Lilly fell asleep.

1

THE DEAD MAN SAT SLUMPED against the rear wall of the small, wood-paneled elevator. His head was resting against his left shoulder, his hands were folded against his chest. Just above his right hand was a blotch of blood. His left leg lay out of the elevator door.

The slippered foot was the first thing Detective Mac Taylor saw as he walked quickly across the marble-tiled lobby of the apartment building on York Avenue near 72nd Street.

Mac moved past two uniformed officers and stood in front of the open door next to Aiden Burn, who was clicking away with her camera at the corpse and the elevator. The dead man was wearing a gray sweat suit with two holes chest high leading into bloody darkness.

"Still snowing?" asked Burn as Mac checked his watch. It was a few minutes after ten. He pulled on a pair of white latex gloves.

"Three more inches expected," said Taylor, kneeling next to the body. There was just enough room for the two Crime Scene Unit investigators and the corpse inside the small elevator.

"Who is he?" Mac asked.

"Name's Charles Lutnikov," Burn said. "Apartment six, third floor."

Lutnikov was about fifty, had thinning dark hair, and a paunch.

"No pockets in the sweat suit," said Mac, gently rolling the body first right and then left. "Who IDed him?"

"Doorman," said Burn, glancing back at the uniformed patrolman who was clearly admiring her rear end.

"You married?" Burn asked the cop, camera in one latex gloved hand.

"Me?" the cop said with a smile, pointing to himself.

"You," she said.

"Yes."

"A man is dead here," she said. "Probable homicide. Look at him, think about him, and not my ass. Can you do that?"

"Yes," said the cop, no longer smiling.

"Good. The kit out there next to the door. Move it just where I can reach it."

"Bad night?" Mac asked.

"I've had better," said Aiden, continuing to snap away as the cop moved Aiden's equipment box.

Mac's eyes were focused on the dead man's chest. "Looks like two bullet holes. No powder burns."

Mac looked at the walls, the floor, the ceiling of

the small wood-paneled elevator and then leaned over and carefully pulled the corpse forward.

"No sign of exit wounds," he said, letting the body slump back.

"Then the bullets are still in him," said Burn.

"No," Mac answered, removing from a leather packet in his pocket a thin steel probe that looked like a dental tool.

He carefully lifted the dead man's shirt to get a better look at the wounds.

"One shot," he said, touching each hole with the probe and talking as much to himself as to Aiden. "This one is an entry wound. Small caliber. It's almost closed. This one is an exit wound, broader, rougher, skin erupted outward."

"Then there should be some blood spatter in front of the body," she said.

"And there they are," said Mac, looking down at dark tear-shaped spots on the floor.

He stood up, put the probe away, took off his latex gloves, dropped them in a bag in his pocket and put on a fresh pair of gloves.

When blood was present, you changed your gloves every time you touched something. No contamination. Criminalists across the world knew that. It took foul-ups in the O.J. Simpson case to make it gospel.

"No gun?" he asked.

"No gun," answered Aiden. "No bullet."

"Body temperature?"

"He's been dead for less than two hours, probably

less than an hour. Doorman found the body and called 911."

Mac gave a final look at the dead man and said, "Photograph his ankles. There's a bruise on this one." Mac pointed to the leg that dangled outside the open door. "Then . . ."

"We go over the walls, floor, sweat suit . . . ?" Aiden asked.

Mac nodded and added, "Full drill."

Full drill included an ALS (Alternate Light Source) examination that would illuminate body fluids including semen, saliva, urine, fingerprints, and even trace narcotics. Aiden had her own compact ALS that fit into a case the size of an eyeglass holder. It plugged into any wall socket, and she used it to check the cleanliness of hotel or motel rooms where she stayed when she was on the road.

Mac moved out of the elevator past the two cops to a man in a purple-and-gold-trimmed doorman's uniform who looked over the officers' shoulders. The man was short and black and very nervous. He had no idea of what to do with his hands so he tried wringing them, then plunged them into his pockets, then took them out again when Mac moved in front of him.

"He's dead," the man said. "I know. I could tell."

"What time did you come on duty, Mr. . . . ?"

"McGee, Aaron McGee. Everyone calls me Mr. Aaron. I mean the tenants do. Don't know why."

"What time did you come on duty, Mr. McGee?"

"Five in the morning." He looked at his watch.

"Five hours ago. Five hours ten minutes. Took me two hours to get here in all that snow."

Mac had his notebook out and was writing carefully.

"Who was on duty before you?"

"Ernesto, Ernesto . . . Let me think. I know it. He's been here five, six years. I know his last name. I'm just, you know?"

Mac nodded.

"You have a sign-in book?" Mac asked.

McGee nodded. "Write in the name of every visitor. Check with the tenant before I let anyone in. Tenants I just write in myself and say 'Good morning' or 'Good night' or some such. Holidays last month, I said 'Merry Christmas' to the ones I know are Christians like me and 'Happy Hanukkah' to the Jews. I don't say anything to the Melvoys. They're atheists, but they give me a little something at Christmas anyway."

"Any visitors for Mr. Lutnikov this morning?"

"Not a one," said the doorman, shaking his head emphatically. "Not for him. Not for anybody in the building. Computer people are supposed to come fix the Rabinowitz's computer this morning."

"Any tenants leave this morning?"

"The Shelbys on ten," said the doorman, motioning for Mac to follow him toward the front door of the Belvedere Towers. "Walked their dog for a few minutes and then came back. Too cold out there for the little thing, but he did his business. Mrs. Shelby was carrying one of those see-through scooper bags, you know. They came back in fast."

Mac nodded.

"And Ms. Cormier," McGee went on. "She goes out every morning, rain, shine, snow, makes no difference. She takes a walk. Eight in the morning. Always says 'Hello, Aaron.' Stays out maybe half an hour, even today."

"She have anything with her?" Mac asked.

"Same as always," McGee said. "One of those big bookstore bags, the kind with a picture of some guy with a beard on it. What's the name of that bookstore?"

"Barnes and Noble?" asked Mac.

"That's it," said McGee. "Same bag every day."

McGee moved with a slight, swaying shuffle. He had to be at least seventy, probably more.

"Sometimes the Glicks will go out early on a Saturday," he said. "They're on two, but he's got the chemotherapy so they've pretty much stayed inside on Saturdays lately."

They stopped in front of the doorman's desk to the right of the front door. Some of the early February freeze seeped through the frame of the door. The snow, at least two feet of it, had stopped falling hours ago, but the temperature was still dropping and more snow was expected. Mac was sure it was now closing in on zero.

His car was parked a block away in a loading zone in front of a deli with his visor pulled down to show his CSI tag. The walk from the car to the apartment building took about five minutes. It would normally have taken no more than a minute or two. It reminded Mac of a wild snowstorm about six years ago in Chicago. In the aftermath of that storm, small, uneven hills of snow had to be climbed like slippery mountains. Mac and his wife lived in a ward in which the alderman was not part of the Democratic Party machine, which meant they were the last to be plowed. It might be days before they could get their car out of the garage. But they had turned the near disaster into a nighttime challenge, climbing, slipping, sliding, falling to make it to the major street four blocks away that had been plowed and where they had found the neighborhood supermarket open.

When Mac slipped on a hill and sank, rear end, into the snow on the way back home, Claire had laughed. Groceries were strewn around him making their own indentations in the snow lit by the hazy streetlights.

Mac hadn't been able to laugh. He looked up with an exaggerated frown, but the frown became a smile. Claire was ankle deep in snow, her ears red, her blue watch cap pulled down to her forehead, her red-knit, gloved hands clutching shopping bags. She was laughing. He could see it all now, dark street, white snow, streetlamp glowing, her laughing.

"Let's see," said McGee. "It's Saturday so the go-to-work people are thinking three times before going out in this weather and it's still early so . . ."

He looked at the book.

"Nothing," he said. "No one else in. No one else's out."

"When's Ernesto's shift?" Mac said, returning fully to the present.

"Midnight to when I come in at five."

McGee looked at the book again, squinting.

"No entries on Ernesto's shift. None at all. No one in. No one out."

An ambulance pulled up outside in front of the door, its sirens silent. Two paramedics dressed in white under blue jackets came out, opened the back door of the ambulance, pulled out a stretcher and a body bag.

The doorman stopped to watch them come in. "I never got any of the names of you policemen," he said. "Maybe I should . . ."

"It's all right," said Mac. "Tell me about Mr. Lutnikov."

"Sorry we're late, Taylor," said the first paramedic through the door, a bodybuilder with a baby face. "Weather."

Mac nodded and said, "Get him to the lab as fast as you can, but be careful out there."

"Roger that," said the bodybuilder, moving with his partner past Mac and the doorman.

"Where were we?" asked McGee as he watched the paramedics track more snow through the lobby.

"Mr. Lutnikov," Mac reminded him.

"Kept to himself mostly," said McGee. "Polite enough. Gave me a fifty dollar bill, crisp, always crisp, on Christmas, every Christmas."

"He had a lot of money?" asked Mac.

"Don't know," said McGee with a smile. "That's about average for Christmas. Everyone in the building gives me cash on the holidays. Want to know how much I got this past holiday? Three thousand four hundred and fifty dollars. Put it right in the bank."

There was a stir of movement down the hallway by the elevators. Mac glanced over. The dead man's leg was still hanging out the door.

"You found the body," said Mac.

"Sure did," said McGee, pointing down the hallway. "Heard the elevator stop, looked over for someone to get out. Nobody did. Bell just kept ding-dinging so I went to look. Know what I saw?"

"A leg sticking out and the door slamming into it," said Mac.

"That's right. That's right. Door's automatic. Stick something out and it just keeps banging against it and ding-dinging."

Which accounted for the bruises on the dead man's ankle. It also suggested that the dead man's leg had been propped against the elevator door and fell out when the door was opened.

"Does the elevator automatically come back down here?"

"No sir. You have to push the L button or it sits wherever it stopped last."

"Are the two other elevators as small as the one with the body?" Mac asked.

"No sir," repeated the doorman. "They're considerably bigger. Elevator three is small because it only goes up from fifteen to the penthouse and then back down here."

A whirl of wind beyond the rattling glass front

doors turned the doorman's head. "Looks real bad out there. Hear it's cold too. Below zero."

"Mr. Lutnikov lived on three," Mac said. "Any idea why he was on an elevator that didn't stop at his floor?"

McGee shook his head. "Everything from fifteenth floor up is single apartments. Take up the whole floor. Four, five bedrooms, balconies. Ms. Louisa Cormier in the penthouse has her own screening room, with these real plush seats and a great big screen. People up there have the big dollars."

"For Lutnikov to get to elevator three . . ." Mac prompted.

"He'd have to come down to the lobby, get on elevator three, and go back up," said the doorman.

"Mr. Lutnikov know anyone who lived on fifteen or above?" asked Mac.

McGee shrugged his bony shoulders.

"Wouldn't know," he said. "Friendly building but not close-like. People in the lobby say hello, smile polite-like but . . ."

The paramedics were coming through the hall carrying a stretcher with a zippered body bag, the dead man inside. Mac could see Aiden Burn putting crime-scene tape across the door of the elevator.

"I'll get the door for you," said McGee, hurrying in front of the paramedics and pushing open the door to a rush of wind, an invading gust of snow and a blast of icy air that ran through Mac's shoulder blades.

Aiden joined Mac. She slipped her gloves off and

dropped them in her pocket. The lingering cold from the outside attack of the storm had hit her. She zipped up her blue jacket, the twin of Mac's with the words "Crime Scene Unit" in white letters across the back.

"He wasn't going out jogging in his slippers," said Mac, watching the body being loaded into the ambulance.

"Where was he going?" asked Aiden.

"Or coming from?" answered Mac.

"Somewhere between fifteen and twenty-one, which is the penthouse," she said. "The buttons show the elevator doesn't go between one and fourteen, but it does go to the lobby and the basement. There's a B button on the elevator. No garage."

"You take the basement. I'll start on fifteen."

"Whoever shot our victim stood outside the elevator," Aiden said. "No powder burns on his shirt. Elevator's too small to fire a shot and leave no powder burn."

Mac nodded.

"And," she added, "he or she was a good shot. Entry wound is right in line with the heart."

"Can I turn elevator three back on?" asked the doorman.

"No," said Mac. "It's a crime scene. There's a stairwell?"

McGee nodded his head and said, "It's the law."

"The tenants will have to use the staircase down to the fifteenth floor and take one of the elevators from there or keep walking," Mac said.

"They are not going to like that," said McGee,

shaking his head. "Not at all. Can I call them and tell them?"

"Right after you give me the names of every tenant from the fifteenth floor up," said Mac.

"I'll write them down for you," said McGee, picking up an automatic pencil from the dark brown desk and clicking it with his thumb.

2

ED TAXX ADJUSTED THE THERMOSTAT in room 614 of the Brevard Hotel. The thermometer showed it was sixty-five degrees, but the Brevard was old, the heating system unreliable, and the weather outside frigid white.

Taxx was a twenty-five-year veteran with the District Attorney's security division. One more year and his daughter would be off to college in Boston. Then, Ed told his wife, they would head for Florida and screw the New York winters.

Ed had grown up on Long Island, had looked forward to winter snows, snowball fights, sledding down Maryknoll Hill, being kid macho like the other boys playing hockey with freezing fingers and ears in Stanton Park. When he reached the age of forty, he stopped looking forward to the winters, the car that threatened not to start, the snow that kept him in his car for hours with the heat turned up, and the need to concentrate to keep from skidding always on his mind. Worst of all were the long gray depressing days. He would not miss the city when he retired.

He looked at Cliff Collier, who didn't look cold at all. Collier was thirty-two, bull strong. He had been an NYPD uniformed officer for six years and a detective for two years.

In two hours they would be relieved by another team guarding Alberta Spanio, who was currently asleep in the locked bedroom. Cliff and Ed had met two nights earlier when they relieved two others from their respective offices. Each night they had tucked Alberta in just before midnight, heard her lock the dead bolt. Collier had spent the night watching television shows constantly being interrupted by weather reports as the snow piled higher and the temperature dropped lower. Taxx had sporadically watched television and read a mystery novel set in Florida.

The two men neither liked nor disliked each other. They had little in common but the job. After ten minutes of small talk once Alberta locked her door, they had settled into conversational silence and Jay Leno as background white noise.

The Brevard Hotel was not a regular safe house for the NYPD or the District Attorney's office. No chances were being taken with Alberta Spanio. No chance that there was a leak in the department. That's what the two men and the people on the other two shifts had been told. They all had enough smarts and experience to be selected for the job, which meant that they all knew there was a chance that the people they were protecting Alberta Spanio from might find out where she was.

Had Alberta, short, big busted, unnaturally blonde,

and very naturally frightened, asked for a phone call, Ed and Cliff would have given her a polite "no," the same polite "no" she would had received if she asked for a ham sandwich. No room service. No outside delivery. Food came in only when there was a shift change.

The relief officers, due in about an hour, would bring something for breakfast, probably Egg McMuffin sandwiches and coffee, which had been their breakfast of choice the day before.

"It's eight," Taxx said, looking at his watch. "We'd better wake her."

"I could use the john," said Collier, who rose from the couch and nodded as he moved to the bedroom door. He knocked loudly and called, "Wake up call, Alberta."

No answer. Collier knocked again.

"Alberta." First a call and then a question, "Alberta?"

Taxx was at his side now. He knocked and shouted, "Wake up."

Still no answer. The two men looked at each other. Taxx nodded at Collier who understood.

"Open it up or we break it down," said Taxx, loud but calmly.

Taxx looked at his watch, counted off fifteen seconds and stepped out of the way so the younger, larger cop could throw his weight against the door. Collier threw his shoulder into the door the way he'd been shown in the Academy. Use the muscle part of the arm not the bony part of the shoulder. Don't throw everything into the first lunge if you

don't have to get in fast. Hit it hard, wear it down.
Fight the wood, not the lock. When Collier hit it, the
door cracked but didn't open. The dead bolt held.
Collier backed up a few steps and threw himself into
the door again. This time it flew open to the sound
of splintering wood, and Collier stumbled forward,
almost falling.

The room was nearly frigid.

Taxx looked at the bed, a mound of blankets. The
window across the room was closed, but a draft of icy
air was coming from the open door of the bathroom.

"Bathroom window," said Taxx, rushing for the
bed.

Collier righted himself and ran the eight or ten feet
across the room to the bathroom. The window was
open, wide open. Collier stepped into the tub to look
out the window over the mound of snow that had
gathered, considered closing the window but stopped
himself, stepped out of the tub, and went back across
the tile to the open door of the bathroom.

Taxx stood next to the bed. He had pulled the
covers back. Collier could see the close-eyed corpse
of Alberta Spanio turned on her side, her face white,
a long-handled knife plunged deeply into her neck.

Ed Taxx and Cliff Collier didn't know Alberta
Spanio and what little they had seen of her they had
not liked. She had no record, no arrests. She had cut
no deal. She had been Anthony Marco's mistress for
three years and was afraid of him. She had wanted
out, and when Marco had been arrested for murder
and racketeering, Alberta had made a call to the District Attorney's office.

If she had second thoughts after telling everything she knew about Anthony, which was a lot, she had settled in to a sullen, surly, and foul-mouthed irritability.

There was no moment of grief for Taxx and Collier, but there was an understanding that their failure to protect a key witness in the murder trial of a major organized crime figure would have consequences that would affect their careers.

There was no phone in the bedroom. It had been removed to keep Alberta Spanio from making any calls. Collier moved quickly into the other room through the broken door and headed for the phone.

Homicide detective Don Flack knew Cliff Collier, not well, but well enough for first names and talks and a cup of coffee from a machine in a precinct hallway when they ran into each other from time to time. They had gone through the Academy together.

Now Collier was District, caught all kinds of calls, from double-dealing prostitutes to gang mayhem. Because of his size, Collier looked intimidating. Because of his nature, he was. Flack knew that because of Collier's ambition—his father and uncle had both been cops—he was worrying about his future as he answered Flack's questions.

Taxx seemed to be more stoic about what had happened. They had lost an important witness in a trial in which she was going to testify in two days. This wasn't the kind of thing that you'd lose your pension over, and Taxx had no further departmental ambitions. What had happened would go in his record. So what? He was not looking for a promotion or a pay raise. Still, he had been on watch when the person he was responsible for had died, not under his nose exactly, but close enough.

Flack had his notebook in hand, the collar of his leather jacket pulled up over his neck to hold back the cold. With the door down and the bathroom window still open, the room in which they were standing seemed to be getting colder by the second despite the rush of warmth from a nearby heating vent.

Inside the bedroom, Detective Stella Bonasera was standing at the side of the bed looking down at the corpse, taking photographs. In the bathroom Danny Messer, wearing latex gloves, called out, "No sign of forced entry."

Stella coughed and felt a slight tickle in her throat. She might be coming down with a cold. Maybe, if she got a chance, she would swallow a couple of aspirin.

She held the camera at her side, looked down at the corpse and resisted the impulse to brush a stray lock of dark-rooted blonde hair from the face of the dead woman. Alberta Spanio had tried hard to hold onto the Brooklyn good looks she'd had ten or twelve years earlier, but she had been losing the battle. The blood had run down her neck and onto the pillow she was resting on, not a lot of blood, at least not a lot compared to what Stella might have expected. She put the camera in her pocket, reached into her CSI kit, took out the magnetic powder container, opened it, removed the powder brush, and carefully checked for prints on the smooth handle of the knife in the woman's neck. Clean. No prints.

On the end table next to the bed were two items of interest. One was an open pill container with two pills left in it. The container was labeled ALEPPO, which Stella knew was a generic name for Sonata. Sheldon Hawkes would tell her how much of the drug was in the dead woman. Stella dusted the container for prints. There was one clear print. She picked up the pill bottle by placing two fingers of her gloved hand inside it, and then she dropped the container and the nearby cap into a plastic bag which she zipped shut and put into her kit on the floor.

The other item on the table was an eight-ounce clear glass with a small amount of amber liquid at the bottom. Stella leaned over to smell the glass. Alcohol. Hawkes would also tell her how much alcohol the dead woman had consumed. A combination of sleeping pills and alcohol could kill, but the knife in Alberta Spanio's neck probably ruled out that option as cause of death.

Stella dusted the glass for prints, found three good ones, poured the liquid into a plastic cup with a screw top she retrieved from her kit and then, after putting the cup in her kit, carefully placed the glass into a plastic envelope and sealed it.

"Want to take a look?" Danny called from the open doorway to the bathroom.

He had already brushed the door handle inside and out for prints, found some, and carefully lifted them.

"Coming," Stella said, stepping back from the bed.
She moved into the bathroom and looked at the open window.

"When did she die?" asked Danny.

Stella shrugged.

"Body's cold, can't be sure, maybe Hawkes can narrow it, but she's not frozen. I'd say the last three hours tops."

"When did the snow stop?" Danny asked.

"I don't know," said Stella. "Four, five hours ago. We'll check it out."

"Killer must have been little," said Danny, looking at the small open window. "Climbed down from above on a ladder or a rope. There's no fire escape out there. Hell of a circus act with the wind and snow."

Stella moved to the window, took a fresh pair of latex gloves from her pocket, put them on, and reached out and ran her fingers across the lower wooden frame. Then she reached out and felt along the outside frame of the window. The cold burned her cheeks and she eased herself back in.

"Take the window to the lab," she said.

"Right," said Danny.

"Check the toilet, too," she said, suppressing a sniffle.

"I did," he answered. "Nothing."

"Then let's both work the other room. I'll check the body, bed, and end table. You do the floor and walls."

"After I remove the window?" he asked.

"The window can wait till we're done," she said.

In the next room, Taxx was saying, "Look for yourself."

He moved to the window and looked out, Flack at his side. Collier simply stood in the middle of the room, looking toward the open bedroom door, his hands fidgeting.

"Six floors up," said Taxx to Flack. "No fire escape."

"None outside the bathroom window?" asked Flack.

Taxx shook his head. "Brick wall," said Taxx. "See for yourself."

"I will," said Flack. "And you didn't hear anything from the bedroom all night?"

"Nothing," said Taxx.

"Nothing," Collier agreed.

"When she went to bed . . . tell me what happened," Flack said.

The pattern, the two officers agreed, had been the same all three nights. Alberta Spanio brought a drink into the bedroom, took two sleeping pills, said "good night" with drink in hand, dead-bolted the lock, and presumably went to bed. There was a television in the bedroom, but the two men guarding her hadn't heard it, and it wasn't on when they broke down the door. They hadn't heard the bath or shower running either though they knew they would have had Alberta used them. She had showered two nights earlier. Besides, they had seen her take the sleeping pills and a long swallow of Scotch. She should have been asleep about a minute after they left her room.

"What the hell happened?" Collier asked, looking toward the bedroom and probably imagining the rest of his life in his current grade, if he was lucky.

Flack didn't give an answer. He knew Collier didn't expect one. He closed his notebook.

3

LUTNIKOV'S APARTMENT WAS SMALL—a living room and a small bedroom with an alcove kitchenette.

The living room was more like a library with books haphazardly filling the floor-to-ceiling cases on three walls. A large wooden desk with a typewriter sat in the middle of the room. The desk, covered with a mess of papers, newspaper clippings, and magazines, faced away from the wide window so the light would come over his shoulder as he worked. The pile on the desk threatened to tumble to the floor, and in fact some of it, three sheets of paper, seemed to have done just that.

There was a recliner chair not far from the desk with a lamp behind it and a small table piled with books next to it. Across from the recliner was a sofa that was soft, brown, in need of repair, and almost but not quite old enough to qualify as a 1950s nostalgia antique.

The only other room in the apartment that the building manager had opened for Aiden and Mac was Lutnikov's bedroom. It contained more bookshelves loaded with books and stacked magazines, a dresser, closet, chest of drawers with a white twenty-seven-inch Sony television on top of it, and a double bed that was blanketed and tucked in military style in contrast to the chaos of the rest of the apartment.

"Kitchen's over there," said the manager, a man named Nathan Gremold, who was in his sixties and well dressed with a wide, bright silvery tie. Gremold was a senior manager for Hopwell and Freed, the third-largest building management company in Manhattan, specializing in upscale apartment buildings. He had been trying not to show his disapproval of Lutnikov's apparent indifference to the high-end dwelling he occupied.

The area he pointed to was not a kitchen but an alcove and it didn't need pointing out.

Aiden and Mac moved across the living room, past the desk to the kitchenette a step behind Nathan Gremold. The kitchen alcove was immaculate. It was more than tidy. It was scrubbed clean, its counter clear, nothing on it but matching wooden salt and pepper shakers.

Mac opened the cupboards. Cartons and cans were neatly aligned. There was one shelf completely devoted to boxes of organic cereal.

"Man liked his cereal," said Aiden.

Mac took out a box, examined it briefly, and put it back.

The refrigerator was well stocked but not overly full. An almost unused carton of vanilla soy milk sat on the top shelf next to a neatly tied half-finished loaf of whole-grain, sprouted bread.

They moved back into the living room where Nathan Gremold hovered, hands at his sides.

"We're fine," said Mac. "We'll lock the door when we're finished. Just two questions," said Mac as Aiden moved to the desk and began looking at the stack of papers and the typewriter.

Gremold hesitated. "Yes," he said.

"Did Mr. Lutnikov own this apartment?" asked Mac.

"No," said Gremold. "It's a rental."

"How much is the rent?"

"Three thousand a month," Gremold said. "This is one of our few economy apartments."

"How did he pay?"

"By check. On the first. Never late."

"Do you know what he did for a living?"

"I checked his original application when the police called our office," Gremold said. "If you'd like a copy . . ."

"We would," said Mac.

"On the application, Mr. Lutnikov said he was a writer, a writer of copy, mostly for the catalogues of high-end clothing and furniture companies."

"Income?" asked Mac.

"As I recall, he said his earnings were $130,000 per year on average."

"Did he list references?"

"I'm sure he did," said Gremold, "but off the top . . ."

"Thanks," said Mac, taking out a card and handing it to Gremold. "Please fax a copy of that application to my office."

"Of course," said Gremold. He took a notebook from his jacket pocket and inserted the card into it.

When he was gone, Mac turned his attention back to the apartment.

"Most of this," Aiden said, looking at the pile on the desk, "looks like notes, some typed."

"What kind of notes?" asked Mac, moving to the bookcase against the wall on his left.

"Like this one," she said, holding up a sheet.

The scribbled note on a blue Post-it read: *Check on poisons. Any that can't possibly be detected?*

"He should have come to us," said Mac, scanning the shelves.

"Odd notes for a guy who writes upscale catalogues," she said, looking deeper into the pile.

"Odd guy," said Mac. "Makes his bed like a marine drill sergeant, keeps his kitchen operating room clean, and works in a mess."

"It's a mess," said Aiden checking a pile of magazines, "but it's clean. You'd think he'd have a computer."

"Throwback," Mac said, not looking up.

He stepped back, looked around, searching for something. There were no file cabinets and he didn't see what he was looking for nearby so he made a slow walk-through of the apartment. About half the books on the shelves were mysteries. The rest were a broad, eclectic spectrum of history, science, geography, and the arts.

When he walked back into the living room from the bedroom, Aiden was going through the drawers of the desk.

"Notice anything that shouldn't be here?" he asked.

She paused, looked around, shook her head, and turned her eyes to him.

"How about something that should be here but isn't?" he asked.

She looked again, and then it struck her.

"He told Gremold he made his living by writing for upscale catalogues," she said.

"You see any catalogues in this apartment?" he asked.

She shook her head.

"Man had no pride in his work," said Aiden.

"Or he didn't make his living writing catalogues," said Mac.

Using the list the doorman Aaron McGee had given him, Mac started on the fifteenth floor. Using a portable ALS in a flashlight and an amber eye shield, he checked the small hallway in front of the elevator carefully for blood, saliva, drug traces, anything he might use. He also searched for, but didn't really expect to find, the murder weapon or the bullet. The killer had probably removed them both, but stranger things had happened, much stranger. He would repeat the procedure on each floor.

The residents of each of the upper seven floors of the building, if they were home, would probably have heard gunshots only if they had been fired on their floor. Probably. The apartments were old with thick walls. Mac wondered if the tenants would have heard a gunshot even if they had been standing in front of the elevator. It would depend, he concluded, on how many floors away the shot had been fired.

Six of the residents, according to the doorman, were wintering in Florida, including the Galleghers on sixteen and the Galleghers on seventeen. The Galleghers on seventeen were the son, daughter-in-law, and grandchildren of the Galleghers on sixteen. Mason and Tess Cooper on nineteen were in California, in Palm Springs. Cooper had told McGee more than once that the house he owned in Palm Springs was right next door to the one that had been owned by Danny Thomas.

That left fifteen, eighteen, twenty, and twenty-one.

Evan and Faith Taft on fifteen were still asleep when Mac used the brass knocker on their door. Evan, in his fifties, blue robe failing to hide a paunch, tousled brown hair, answered the door, and blinked when Mac showed him his badge.

"What's wrong?" asked Taft.

"Someone was killed in your elevator, Mr. Taft," said Mac.

"In our elevator?"

"Did you hear any shots or unusual noises this morning?"

"Someone was shot in this building? In our elevator?"

"Yes," said Mac. "Did you hear anything?"

"No," said Taft. "I'm going to have to tell my wife. Oh, shit, she's got a heart problem. We'll probably have to sell the apartment and move. She won't want to go on that elevator again. You know what the housing market's like in this city?"

Mac waited while Evan Taft sighed and continued.

"Maybe we'll stay at our place on the Island. If we can get to it with all this snow."

"Do you know Charles Lutnikov, who lives in this building?" asked Mac.

"Name doesn't . . . Did he kill someone?"

"No, he was the victim."

"What floor is he on?"

"Three. Heavy-set man, slightly balding, maybe a little unkempt."

"I don't know, maybe," said Taft. "Sounds familiar but . . ."

"I'll have someone come by with a photograph of him later," said Mac. "How well do you know the rest of your neighbors, the ones who use this elevator?"

"Not well," he said. "The Wainwrights on eighteen, he's the Wainwright of Rogers and Wainwright, the stock brokers. He handles some of our investments. The others, we don't know them very well, enough to say hello if we meet on the elevator or in the lobby. The Barths on twenty are retired, Redwear cardboard cartons factory in North Carolina. The Coopers on nineteen, you know the Daisy Ice Cream chain in the South?"

"No," said Mac.

"Well, the Cooper family owns them," said Evan, brushing back his hair and looking over his shoulder to see if his wife was coming. "Big family."

"Top floor, penthouse? Louisa Cormier?" asked Mac.

"Our celebrity," said Taft. "She's on the *Times* Best Seller list again. Nice enough lady. You know, elevators in passing, 'How are you,' that kind of thing. Keeps to herself."

"Yes," said Mac. "Did you hear any noise this morning, probably just before eight?"

"Noise?"

"Like a gunshot," said Mac.

"No, our bedroom is in the back of the apartment. Anything else?"

"No," said Mac.

"Then I'd better go figure out how to tell my wife."

Mac nodded. Taft closed the door.

Mac had no better luck on any of the other floors. Aiden caught up with him on twenty-one, and they went over the foyer together as he had on the lower floors. When they were finished, Aiden vacuumed the floor, as she had every other one, and put the vacuumed contents in a separate marked see-through plastic bag.

Before Mac tapped the shining brass knocker on Louisa Cormier's door, he used an ALS to examine the foyer. There were small but definite traces of blood.

4

DR. SHELDON HAWKES, lean, dark-skinned wearing blue jeans and a black T-shirt with the letters CSI across the back, stood between the tables bearing the two corpses. Standing at his side was Stella Bonasera.

The sparse room was large, with blue-tinted light and slightly shadowed corners. The only bright lights were those which shone down from the ceiling, white beams on the two naked and tagged stars of the day, Alberta Spanio, knife still in her neck, and Charles Lutnikov, the two holes in his chest now clearly visible. Both bodies were nude on the steel tables, devoid of jewelry, going out of the world as they had come in with the exception of the autopsy, their eyes closed, their heads on stabilizing blocks.

Hawkes had checked the temperature of both bodies the moment they had arrived and compared them with the rectal temperatures Stella and Aiden had taken. Time of death was never 100 percent accurate unless there happened to be a witness standing there when it happened and you had full trust in the witness and his or her wristwatch. Rigor mortis had not set in on either body, which suggested the deaths were less than eight hours ago. "Suggested" was the operative word since Alberta Spanio's body had been first examined by Stella in a room in which the temperature was 22°F.

Rigor mortis, however, is a highly unreliable predictor of time of death. Rigor mortis is the stiffening and contraction of muscles resulting from chemical reactions in muscle cells. Normally, rigor begins in the face and neck and works down through each muscle till even those in the corpse's toes are affected. Rigor usually begins eighteen to thirty-six hours after death and lasts about two days when the muscles relax and begin to decompose. Heat quickens the process. Hawkes had seen it in bodies which had only been dead for a few hours. Cold slows down the process. Hawkes remembered cases in which rigor did not take place for a week. In thin people it could come on rapidly regardless of temperature. In obese people, the process would be much slower than the norm. And then again it was not unusual for a body to never show signs of rigor.

Hawkes concluded, without beginning his autopsies, that the time of death calculated by the CSI detectives at the site of the killings might be reasonably accurate. Normal body temperature is 98.6°F. At the rate of approximately 1.5°F per hour, the body equilibrates with the temperature of the environment in which the body has been found unless the temperature of the environment is very hot or extremely cold. Given the 72°F temperature in the elevator and the dead man's temperature, it was relatively easy to

determine Charles Lutnikov's time of death; it had
been harder, much harder, with Alberta Spanio because of the partial freezing which would have
dropped her body temperature rapidly. Hawkes
could make a better estimate of time of death if he
began with her and examined her systems and organs with his own instruments.

He began with the knife sticking out of her neck.

"Downward stroke," he said carefully, removing
the knife. "Deep. Someone strong. Also someone
lucky or someone who knew just where the carotid
artery was. She was asleep. No struggle. No movement. Not even after she was stabbed. Knife is a
switchblade right out of *The Blackboard Jungle* or *West
Side Story* which shows you how up-to-date I am
about movies. Cheap, sharp."

Hawkes dropped the bloody knife into a stainless
steel pan and handed it to Stella. She would add it to
the collection, which included the pill bottle and lid
and the glass with alcohol from the hotel room. By
the time Hawkes finished, the bathroom window
might also be in the lab waiting for her.

Hawkes moved into the routine autopsy procedure which always seemed new and sacred, not the
defiling of the dead but the honoring of justice
which they and their families deserved.

Hawkes carefully made a Y incision, a cut into the
body from shoulder to shoulder, meeting at the ster-
num and then going straight down the abdomen to
the pelvis.

The interior organs were now exposed. Hawkes
used a standard tree-branch looper to cut through

the ribs and collarbone. He lifted the rib cage away to expose the heart and other soft organs which he took out and weighed. The next step was to take samples of fluid from all the organs, followed by making a slit in the exposed stomach and intestines to examine the contents.

When his examination of the torso was complete, Hawkes moved to Alberta Spanio's head, first probing the eyes for hemorrhages in case the victim was strangled before she was stabbed. Then he carefully made an incision in the scalp behind the head and peeled the skin forward over the face to expose the skull. With a high-speed oscillating power saw, he cut through the skull and opened it with a chisel, prying off the skullcap so he could lift out the brain in order to weigh and examine it without doing it any damage.

As he engaged in each step, he described what he was doing and what he saw. His words were recorded, and the tape labeled as evidence.

"Done," he said finally. "I'll get the samples to the lab."

"Tell them it has to be done quickly," said Stella. "I'll prod them from our end." It was not uncommon in New York for a homicide lab report to drag on for weeks or even months.

Hawkes nodded and moved to the sink in the corner where he took off his bloody gown and gloves, washed, and put on fresh gloves.

Stella felt light-headed, and it must have shown because Hawkes said, "You all right?"

"Fine," she said.

It wasn't the autopsy or the sight of the flayed corpse that was getting to her. It was the damn flu. She cursed the weakness, thanked Hawkes, and headed for the door.

"Now," said Hawkes behind her, "let's have a talk with Mr. Lutnikov."

Fortunately for Stella, Lutnikov was Aiden and Mac's case. She wondered why one of them wasn't there.

Detective Don Flack had checked with the front desk and found out who had been in the rooms a floor up and a floor down from the one in which Alberta Spanio had been murdered. To be sure he also checked who had been in the rooms two floors up and two floors down.

The only potentially promising room turned out to be the one directly over the open bathroom window. It had been occupied by a Wendell Lang who had specifically asked for that room two days before and was told it was occupied. He had taken another room, paid cash, and moved into the one over Alberta Spanio as soon as it was vacated. Mr. Lang had checked out at six this morning.

Unfortunately, the clerk Flack got the information from had not been on duty when Wendell Lang checked in or out.

Flack took the original of the sign-in card, holding it carefully in the corners, and dropped it into a small plastic bag which he pocketed. Then, with a key provided by the manager, he went up to the room Wendell Lang had rented.

The room was small. The maid had already made it up. He found the maid with a cart in the hallway, showed his badge, and asked if she had vacuumed the room and if she still had the trash from the room.

The woman, Estrella Gomez, was chubby, fair skinned, and in her thirties. She had only a slight accent when she said, "Room 704. Nothin' in the trash. No newspapers, nothin' in the room. Didn't use the towels. Didn't even sleep in the bed. I ran the vacuum. Tha's all."

Flack told Estrella Gomez to go to the front desk and tell them not to let anyone have the room, that it was a potential crime scene. Then he went back inside the room that Wendell Lang had rented, went to the window, opened it, and looked down and out. Sheer drop and two problems. The window was clearly in view of anyone looking up from 51st Street or across the street from a high-rise office building. The chances of someone lowering himself from the window and not being seen were poor even at night, although Don Flack had seen stranger things.

Flack would know after Hawkes's examination just when Alberta Spanio was murdered. If the sun had already come up, someone climbing out of a sixth-story hotel room stood a more-than-even chance of being spotted.

As he pulled his head back inside the open window, Flack saw a mark in the center of the sill, a small indentation that cut a narrow band through the center of the white wood. The indentation looked new, the exposed wood clean. He touched it, confirmed it was fresh. He took out his cell phone and called Stella.

Just as he was about to knock at Louisa Cormier's door, Mac's cell phone rang. He didn't recognize the caller number on the screen.

"Yes," he said, stopping and looking at the highly polished dark wood door finely engraved with curlicues and flowered vines.

"Mr. Taylor?" came a woman's soft voice.

Aiden stood nearby, aluminum case in hand, waiting.

"Yes," Mac said.

"This is Wanda Frederichson. We'd like to postpone finishing until the weather clears and we can remove enough snow."

Mac said nothing.

"Of course if you want to go ahead on Monday anyway, we'll do our best but we recommend . . ."

"Monday," Mac said. "It has to be Monday. Just do your best."

"And you still want everything we discussed."

"Yes," said Mac. "Long-range weather forecast says there won't be any more snow after tomorrow for at least a week."

"But," said Wanda Frederichson, "the temperature is scheduled to remain around zero for at least seven days."

Mac could tell that the woman wanted to say more, wanted to convince him to wait, but there was no waiting. It had to be Monday.

"And you did say there would be no guests?" Wanda Frederichson asked, double checking.

"None," said Mac. "Just me."

"Ten A.M., Monday then," Wanda Frederichson said, sounding resigned.

Mac flipped his cell phone closed. His eyes met Aiden's. If there was a question behind her brown eyes, she hid it. She knew better than to ask.

Mac used the knocker on the decorated door. From inside the apartment, he could hear five notes chiming.

"Phantom of the Opera," he said.

"Never saw it," she said.

The door opened. A petite woman in her fifties in a white blouse and blue skirt stood before them. Her hair was short, curled, and honey blonde, her eyes blue. Both the color of her hair and eyes were artificial, but nearly perfect. She wasn't quite pretty, but she had a delicate, made-up elegance and an almost sad smile that displayed perfect white teeth.

"Louisa Cormier?" asked Mac.

The woman looked at Mac and Aiden and said, "The police, yes. I was expecting you. Mr. McGee called from downstairs. Please come in."

"I'm Detective Taylor," Mac said. "This is Detective Burn. She'll wait for me out here."

Louisa Cormier looked at Aiden.

"She would be more than welcome . . ." Louisa began and then looked at Aiden's jacket and said, "Crime scene. The young lady is going to go over my foyer."

Mac nodded.

"It's perfectly fine with me," Louisa said with a smile. "Not that I could do anything about it even if it weren't. There's been a murder, and as the most isolated dweller in this building I'd like you to find out who did it as soon as possible. Please come in."

She stepped back so Mac could enter. When he was inside, she closed the door.

The room was more than a room. It was a dark, marble-floored, broad expanse with a dining area bigger than Mac's apartment, with a massive wooden table and sixteen chairs around it, plus a living area that looked large enough to play tennis in furnished with brightly upholstered antique furniture. Sliding glass doors led to a balcony with a panoramic view of the city facing north.

"It is big, isn't it," Louisa said, following Mac's eyes. "This is the part I let *Architectural Digest* use, this and the kitchen, and my library/office. My bedroom however . . ." she pointed toward a door in the living room area, "was off-limits to *Architectural Digest*, but not to you."

"I'd be very interested in seeing all the rooms," Mac said.

"I understand," said the woman with a smile. "Doing your job. Coffee?"

"No, thank you. Just a few questions."

"About Charles Lutnikov," she said, leading him into the living area and, with a delicate right hand, inviting him to sit where he wished.

Mac sat in an upright upholstered chair. Louisa Cormier sat across from him on a claw-legged sofa.

"You knew Mr. Lutnikov?"

"A little," she said. "Poor man. Met him when he first moved in. He was carrying one of my books, had no idea I lived here. I have a well-deserved reputation for being unwilling to talk about my work, but when I saw Charles in the lobby several weeks later he was carrying another of my books. *Vanity.*"

"He was vain?" asked Mac.

"No," she said with a sigh. "That's the title of the book and the main character. I was, however, succumbing to vanity when I saw Charles with one of my books. I asked him if he was enjoying it and he said he was a big fan. Then I told him who I was. For an instant he didn't believe me and then he opened his book to the inside back flap and looked at the photograph. I know what you're thinking, that he knew who I was all the time, but he didn't. I could tell. My only concern was that he not become a gushing fan. I couldn't live with a gushing fan in the same building. You know, afraid to run into him, having to make small talk. The people in this building have respected my privacy as I've respected theirs."

"So you . . . ?"

"Laid out ground rules," she said. "I'd sign his books. He was not to approach me with questions or comments if we ran into each other. We would simply smile and say 'hello.' "

"And it worked?"

"Perfectly."

"Did he ever come up here?" Mac asked.

"Up here? No. Have you ever read any of my books?"

"No, I'm sorry," he said.

"You needn't be. Millions, however, have."

She smiled broadly.

"Someone in our unit is a fan," Mac said. "I've seen him with your books. Did you hear a shot fired this morning?"

"What time?" she asked.

"Probably around eight," he said.

"I was out at eight," she said seriously. "I go out every morning."

"Where did you go this morning?"

"Well, in good weather I walk to Central Park, but this was not the day for it," she said. "I bought a newspaper, had coffee at Starbucks, and came home. Please."

She stood up and headed for the room which she had said was her office/library.

"Come," she said. "I'll sign a book for your police officer friend. The new one, *Courting Death*. It comes out in about a month."

Mac rose to follow her and said, "Did you hear any noise this morning?"

"No," she said, opening the door to the office/library. "No, but I probably wouldn't even if someone were shot right outside my front door. I was in my office here from six till eight with the door closed, working on a new book, and then I went out."

"You took the elevator?" asked Mac.

"You mean did I see a dead man on the elevator?" she asked. "No I did not. I didn't use the elevator. I walked down."

"Twenty-one flights," Mac said flatly.

"Twenty," she said, "we have no thirteenth floor. I walk down the stairs every morning and after my walk, I climb the stairs. Those stairs and my walk are really the only physical exercise I get."

The library/office was big, not as expansive as the rest of the apartment, but big enough for an ornate ebony desk with curved legs and inlaid ivory strips with a matching chair and two walls covered with shelves of books, not as many as Lutnikov had in his smaller apartment, but a sizeable number. Against another wall was a floor-to-ceiling glass-enclosed case with wooden shelves. Neatly stacked on the shelves was an odd assortment of objects.

"My collection," Louisa Cormier said with a smile. "Things I've used for research for my books. I try to use or at least handle crucial objects so I know what I'm talking about."

Mac looked over the collection which included an old Arvin radio from the 1940s, a Boy Scout axe, a large crystal ashtray, an enormous bound book with a red cloth cover, an Erté art deco statue of a sleekly dressed and coiffed woman about a foot high, a claw hammer with a dark wooden handle, a blue decorative pillow with yellow tassels and the words NEW YORK WORLD'S FAIR printed on the front, a two-foot scimitar with a gold handle, a Coke bottle from the 1940s, and dozens of other odd pieces.

"I've been told," Louisa said, "that if I signed them and put them on eBay the collection would be worth close to a million dollars from loyal fans."

"No guns," observed Mac.

"I go to gun shops and firing ranges when I write about guns," she said. "I don't collect them."

There was a set of six file drawers, also ebony, against the wall behind the desk. On the wall above the file cabinets were fourteen framed awards and an eleven-by-fourteen-inch black-and-white photograph of a pretty young girl standing in front of a cleaning store.

"That was me," she said. "My father was the clerk in the store. I worked there after school and on Saturdays. That was back in Buffalo. We were far from well-to-do which turned out to be a blessing since I enjoy and appreciate having and spending money. Here it is."

She was at an eye-level shelf in the right-hand corner of the room. She pulled out a book, opened it to the title page, and asked, "Who is it for?"

"Sheldon Hawkes," Mac said.

She wrote with a slight flourish, closed the book, and handed it to Mac.

"Thanks," he said taking the book.

There was a computer, a Macintosh, on the desk and a printer, no scanner, no state-of-the-art accessories.

"Anything else?" she asked folding her hands, her smile broad, warm.

"Nothing now," said Mac. "Thanks for your time."

She ushered him to the front door and opened it. Aiden stood in the hallway, metal case in one hand.

"If I can be of any further help . . ." said Louisa Cormier.

"Do you have any hired help?" Mac asked.

"No," she said. "A cleaning crew comes in and cleans every three days."

"Secretary?" he asked.

Louisa cocked her head slightly to the left like a frail curious bird and said, "Ann Chen. She keeps my social and business calendar, protects me from reporters, fans, and the idly curious, and handles my correspondence and Web page."

"She work here?" asked Mac.

"Not usually. Normally she works out of her apartment in the Village. My phone number is unlisted but somehow people get hold of it. The calls go to Ann who with a simple touch of a button forwards them to me after she screens them."

Both Aiden and Mac could see that Louisa was definitely considering a question, but decided not to ask it.

"Is that it?" she said instead.

Aiden opened the stairway door. The crime-scene elevator was still on the first floor.

"For now," said Mac with a smile. "I'm sure Sheldon will appreciate the book."

Mac held the book up. He followed Aiden through the door, and they stepped out, leaving Louisa smiling behind them.

When the door closed, Aiden said, "Hawkes reads mysteries?"

"Don't know," said Mac, starting down the narrow stairs. "Give me a large bag. I want to check our famous author's fingerprints. You got blood samples from the carpet?"

Aiden nodded.

"Now," said Mac, "let's see if they match Charles Lutnikov's."

"She know something?" asked Aiden, her voice echoing as they moved slowly downward.

Mac shrugged and said, "She knows something. She was very bubbly, talked too much, kept changing the subject. She was working hard to be a thoughtful hostess with nothing to hide."

"But she lied," said Aiden. Mac had a sense about falsehood. Those who worked with him had learned, sometimes the hard way, not to lie to Mac.

"Everyone lies when they talk to the police," Mac had once told her.

"You find anything?" he asked her now.

As they entered the lobby, Aiden removed a small plastic container from her jacket pocket and handed it to Mac. He held it up to the light to look at the contents.

"What is it?" he asked.

"Six small pieces of paper," she said. "White, like confetti. Found them in the carpeting outside Louisa Cormier's door."

5

ON THE TABLE in front of Stella and Flack lay the pill bottle, the bathroom window, and the drinking glass taken from the hotel bedroom where Alberta Spanio was murdered.

Stella had checked for fingerprints. There were clear ones on the glass and the pill container, all belonging to the dead woman. There were no prints on the bathroom window, but Stella hadn't had the window removed with any real hope of getting reasonable prints. What she wanted was reasonable answers.

"That's the outside of the window. See that hole?" she said to Flack.

She pointed at something on the window. It was hard to miss. The inch-long gash was shaped like a comet and was the color of untreated wood.

"I checked the inside of the hole," she said. "Screw grooves. Something had been screwed into that window and ripped out, leaving that tail-like mark in the wood." Using an extruder gun, Stella had taken a casting that showed even, minute grooves.

At that point, Danny Messer, wearing a white lab coat, came in with two microscope slides and handed them to Stella saying, "The scraping I took out of the screw hole in the window."

Stella inserted the first slide into the microscope and examined it as Danny said, "Iron oxide. Whatever was screwed in there was iron, almost new."

Stella moved to the side to let Flack look at the slide. He did and saw little dark chips in no particular arrangement. When he moved away from the microscope, she inserted the second slide, the one from the room above Alberta Spanio's. She looked for a few seconds and made room for Flack. More chips, but these looked different from the ones on the other slide.

"Steel," said Danny. "Taken from the particles Detective Flack took from the groove in the window above Alberta Spanio's bathroom. They don't match the iron in whatever was screwed into the window."

"And what do you make of that," asked Flack.

"Nothing more than whoever dangled that steel object out the window," Danny said, "had to have something heavy pulling at him on the other end to make a groove like that in the sill."

"A kid?" asked Flack.

"A kid was lowered to the window, went through, and stabbed Alberta Spanio in the neck?" asked Stella.

"I've known kids on the street who'd do it for a

few hundred dollars," said Flack. "And maybe it was a woman, skinny, maybe wasted from drugs, willing to risk her life for drug money."

"How about this?" said Danny. "Someone lowered a chain from the window above Spanio's bathroom with a hook on the end. The hook fit into another hook or hoop screwed into Spanio's bathroom window. He pulled the window open and kept pulling till the screwed-in hoop came out, leaving the hole."

"And then someone climbed down the chain?" asked Flack.

"Possible," said Danny. "Or they were lowered."

"Dangerous," said Flack. "Climbing down a steel chain."

"In a snowstorm," added Danny.

"And then climbing or swinging through the window," said Flack. "Hard for a kid or a druggie."

Stella felt weak, tired. She wanted to put her head down on the table and get an hour of sleep. Instead she said, "Let's go take a closer look at that room above Spanio's bathroom window."

Spread out on the stainless steel table in front of Dr. Sheldon Hawkes was the body of Charles Lutnikov. There was a clean long incision from just below the dead man's neck to just below his stomach. The flap created by the incision was open and deep, dark red surrounding exposed ribs.

Viscera lay open, chest cavity cracked and open like a large book. The light above the corpse left no shadows, exposed every twist of colon and curve of bone and artery.

The room felt slightly colder to Mac than usual, for which he was grateful. The aroma of whatever the dead man had eaten that morning or the night before wafted through the room. Mac looked at Hawkes, who had both hands on the table across from Mac.

"Man had a pizza for breakfast," said Hawkes. "Meatball, eggplant, and onion."

"Interesting," said Mac.

"We start with the easy stuff," said Hawkes. "What do you know about our man?"

"His fingerprints were matched in the military database," said Mac. "Lutnikov served four years in the United States Army in the Military Police. Served in the first Gulf War. Purple Heart."

Hawkes pointed to a scar on the dead man's leg, just above the ankle.

"Probably a land mine," he said. "Still a few small fragments of shrapnel. Surgeon probably decided not to probe for them and cause more trauma. Probably a good decision."

"What about the shot that killed him?"

Hawkes reached down and closed the left side of the chest cavity like the cover of a book.

"Wound that killed him came from a handgun, judging from the size of the wound, a small caliber, probably a .22. Bullet went straight into the heart, almost no angle. He was standing in front of the shooter, who either knew what he or she was aiming for, or got lucky."

Mac nodded and leaned forward to examine the wound.

"Aiden ran a blood splatter drop from the floor of the elevator," said Mac. "Blood from the wound dropped four feet six inches."

"Dead man is five ten and a fraction," said Hawkes.

"So, since the bullet went straight in, Lutnikov was standing up," said Mac.

"And . . . ?" asked Hawkes.

"If the shooter was standing straight up with the weapon held out . . ." Mac went on.

"The shooter was about five foot one or two," Hawkes continued. "Want to hear about the flight of the bullet?"

Mac nodded.

"Bullet went through the heart, took a turn, hit a rib, turned around and came back out a few inches from the entry wound."

Hawkes produced a thin metal trajectory rod like a magician and inserted it in the entry wound. "As I said, and your blood-splatter test confirms, it went straight in."

Hawkes produced another trajectory rod that he inserted into the exit wound at a sharp angle upward, carefully following the path of the bullet through the chest cavity.

Hawkes pulled out the rods and said, "You found no bullet?"

"Not yet," Mac confirmed. "You find anything else?"

Hawkes reached under the table and came up

with a small see-through plastic zip bag. He handed
it to Mac, who held it up and looked at Hawkes.

"Came from wound one," said Hawkes. "Small
pieces of bloody paper."

"Aiden got some of those same fragments at the
crime scene," Mac said. "The bullet must have gone
through paper before it hit Lutnikov."

"A lot of paper," said Hawkes. "Assuming some of
the paper burned on impact, that still leaves the
pieces Aiden found and the ones I've been able to
dig out so far."

"A book?" asked Mac.

"Your problem," said Hawkes, reopening the chest
flap. "But a few of those fragments have ink on
them. Oh, yeah, Lutnikov's blood and the sample
you took in front of the elevator at Louisa Cormier's
apartment. Perfect match."

Five minutes later, Mac Taylor's cell phone rang
while he stood over Aiden's shoulder in the lab
where she was looking through a microscope at the
bloody paper fragments.

"Taylor," he said.

"Mr. Taylor, this is Wanda Frederichson again. I'm
sorry to bother you, but I talked to Mr. Melvin in the
office and he said Monday is impossible. We won't
be able to get a crew in to plow the snow, and the
driveways will be . . ."

"What if someone dies," Mac said.

Aiden looked up from her microscope. Mac
stepped away from her and across the room.

"Pardon?"

"What do you do if someone dies between now and Monday?" asked Mac.

"Do you really . . . ?"

"Yes."

"We keep the bodies refrigerated," she said.

"What about Jews?" asked Mac.

"Jews?"

"They have to bury their dead within a day or two, don't they," he said.

"That's really a question for our Jewish director, Mr. Greenberg," she said.

"I'd like to talk to Mr. Greenberg," Mac said.

"Please Mr. Taylor," Wanda Frederichson said patiently. "I know . . ."

"Detective Taylor," he said. "Do you have a number for Mr. Greenberg?"

"I can connect you," she said with a sigh.

"Thank you," said Mac, looking at Aiden, who was doing her best not to pay attention.

There was a double ring and then another double ring and a man's voice, "Arthur Greenberg, can I help you?"

Mac explained the situation to him and Greenberg listened quietly.

"Let me take a look," Greenberg said. "Take me a few seconds to access my file here on the computer. Normally, I wouldn't be here on Shabbat, but we had a . . . Let's see. We've never had . . . Yes. Mr. Taylor, I'm reading the circumstances in your file. We'll get it done."

Mac gave Greenberg his cell phone number,

thanked him, and clicked the phone shut, moving back toward Aiden.

She looked up at him, showing her curiosity. He ignored it.

"What've we got?" he asked.

"You okay?"

"I'm fine," he said. "What've we got?"

"What we don't have is a weapon or a bullet," she said. "What we do have are pieces of heavy duty, white bond paper A4 size, 80gm/2, acid free non-erasable. They match the paper in Lutnikov's apartment."

"And some of the paper you and Hawkes found in the entry wound had ink on them. What about the paper fragments you found outside Louisa Cormier's apartment?"

Aiden nodded and said, "Match. It doesn't prove she shot him, but it suggests that the shot that killed Lutnikov was fired from just outside Louisa Cormier's elevator door. But there are lots of ways those six fragments could have gotten onto Louisa Cormier's foyer carpet. We might even have tracked them in on the bottom of our shoes."

"No," said Mac.

"No," Aiden agreed.

"But," said Mac. "A good lawyer . . ."

"And Louisa Cormier can afford the best," added Aiden.

Mac nodded and said, "A good lawyer could give a lot of explanations. See if you can match any of those ink spots with Lutnikov's typewriter."

He stood silently for a few seconds before speaking again.

"How tall would you say Louisa Cormier is?"

Aiden looked up, thought for an instant, and said, "Maybe five two. Why?"

Before he could answer, she said, "The blood splatter."

"The blood splatter," he confirmed, telling her about his conversation with Sheldon Hawkes and Hawkes's conclusion about the wound.

"Lutnikov was carrying paper he had typed on when he was shot," said Mac. "The bullet went through the paper. He was holding it against his chest."

"For protection," said Aiden.

"Against a bullet?"

"It was all he had," she said.

"Maybe he was trying to protect what he had written," said Mac. "Maybe he was killed for it."

"Then where is whatever he wrote?" she said. "And where's the bullet . . ."

"And the gun," added Mac. "You know what we do next."

Aiden got up.

"I put on my coat, make my way across the wild north, and come back with a typewriter ribbon."

"And . . ." Mac began.

"More samples of paper in Lutnikov's apartment," she finished. "Samples he typed on."

"Take a vacuum," said Mac. "Go over the floor on every level outside the elevator for trace."

"We already did," she said.

"But now we know what we're looking for," said Mac.

Aiden nodded knowingly. "The murder weapon, the bullet that killed Lutnikov, whatever he was carrying when he was shot and . . ."

"A motive," said Mac.

"I'd better get going," she said.

6

THE MAID HAD CONFIRMED that the man who had
rented the hotel room for the night had not used the
bed, and that she had not touched it at all this morning. Looking at the bed while Danny Messer crawled
on his hands and knees on the floor, Stella Bonasera
was sure the man had not even sat on the bed.

The two of them had examined the few pieces of
furniture in the room—bed, chair and small desk,
cabinet containing three drawers and holding a
small color television—the door handle, even the
rod and walls in the small closet. They hadn't found
what they were looking for.

Stella moved to the window.

Don Flack had interviewed the rest of the hotel
staff, including the clerk who had been on duty the
day before when Wendell Lang had checked into the
room. The man had paid in cash in advance with
two hundred dollars extra to cover phone calls or
use of the refrigerator/bar. He had made no phone
calls, had not used the bar, and had not bothered to
pick up his two hundred. He had simply checked out

electronically. The clerk hadn't been able to give a good description of the man.

"It was storming," the clerk had told Flack. "He had his hat down and a scarf around his chin. He was big. I can tell you that. Big. At least two hundred and fifty pounds, probably quite a bit more. The other man was small, very small."

"Other man?" asked Flack.

"Yes," said the clerk. "I think they were together. The other man stood back, hands in his coat pocket. He had his collar turned up and his hat, one of those old Fedora types, was pulled down."

"But this Wendell Lang who took the room only signed for himself, one person?" asked Flack.

"Yes," said the clerk, "but it didn't matter. Double and single occupancy cost the same. The room is a single. One bed. They were an odd-looking pair, one huge, one small."

One who didn't weigh much and one who could hold the little man's weight at the end of a steel link chain, Don had thought. He'd immediately gone back up to the room and related his encounter with the clerk to Stella. She nodded in acknowledgement and kept working.

Stella examined the window sill from which Don Flack had taken the sliver sample of steel. She dusted the inside of the window and the handle for prints and then opened it. She leaned out into the frozen air and dusted the outside of the window. She pulled the tapes with the prints into the room and closed it.

"I'll have to remove the carpet," Danny said from

where he knelt on the floor. Stella turned to him. Danny, white-gloved hands rubbing together, looked as if he were praying.

"Do it," she said.

Danny nodded, got up, moved to the wall near the door with his toolbox, found a hammer, and went to work. Neither he nor Stella expected to find anything under the carpet, but they were looking for something specific or for some evidence that what they were looking for didn't exist.

"I'm going back to the lab to check out the fingerprint and see what I can find about whatever made that rut in the window sill. "You want to come?" she asked Flack, who declined, saying he would exhaust all possible leads at the hotel.

Danny nodded. In his left hand he held a high power-trace, evidence-collection vacuum. In the vacuum was an evidence bag designed for one-time use. The room wasn't large. Stella knew that tearing up the carpet should take him no more than an hour if he was lucky. On a normal day, he would probably have time after that to go home and shower, but the snow and slow traffic would mean at least an additional hour.

As the first strip of carpeting pulled away from the floor revealing an assortment of dead bugs, including a flattened black roach, Stella said, "Call me when you know either way."

"Right," he grunted.

Aiden and Mac met a very agitated Ann Chen at Whitney's in the Village. She wasn't hard to spot, the

Asian woman coming into the almost-empty coffee house alone soon after them.

When she came through the door bringing a rush of frigid air in with her, she looked around and saw the two CSI investigators sitting at a table in the corner, coffee mugs before them. Mac held up a hand, and Ann Chen acknowledged him with a nod of her head. She peeled off her coat and woolen cap revealing an oversized, thick, white turtle-neck woolen sweater underneath. She dropped the coat and hat on the empty seat next to Aiden.

"Coffee?" asked Mac.

"Espresso, double," she said.

Mac placed the order by calling over to the young man a few feet away behind the counter.

Ann Chen was thin, about thirty, pretty but not beautiful. She was also clearly nervous, shifting frequently in her chair in a fruitless effort to get comfortable.

"I usually sleep late on weekends," she said. "Unless Louisa needs me."

"Does she need you a lot on weekends?"

"Not really," said Ann. "Mr. Lutnikov is really dead?"

"You knew him?" asked Aiden.

Ann shrugged as the young man brought her double espresso. Mac handed him three dollar bills.

"I saw him around the building," Ann said, cradling the hot cup in her lean fingers.

"Did he ever come to Ms. Cormier's apartment?" asked Mac.

Ann looked down and said, "I've got to tell you

I'm uncomfortable with this. Louisa has been so good to me that . . . I'm not comfortable with this."

"Did she call you this morning?" asked Mac.

Ann nodded.

"She said I could expect to hear from the police. Then you called."

"Was there anything she asked you not to tell us?" Mac asked.

"No," said Ann vehemently.

"What do you do for Louisa?" asked Aiden.

"Correspondence, set up radio and television interviews, print interviews, signings, tours," said Ann. "Pay bills, answer Website E-mail."

"You don't work on her manuscripts?" asked Mac.

"Yes, when they're finished. On some days I arrive at the apartment and she says something like, 'The new one's done.' Then she hands me a floppy disk, and I take it to the computer at the back of the apartment off of the kitchen and copyedit it. They're usually in good shape though, and there's not much to do. It's still a thrill to be the first one to read a new Louisa Cormier mystery."

"Then?" asked Aiden.

"Then I tell Louisa I'm done and I love the book, because I always do."

"And how does she respond?" asked Mac.

"She usually smiles, says 'Thank you dear' or something like that and takes the floppy.

"I was an English major at Bennington," said Ann Chen after another sip of coffee. "I've got two novels of my own finished. I've spent the last three years trying to decide if I should ask Louisa to read them. She might not like them. She might think I took the job with her just to get her to help my writing career. I did try a few times to let her know that I wanted to be a writer. She never picked up on it."

"How tall are you?" asked Aiden.

Ann looked surprised.

"How tall? About five two."

"Ms. Cormier have a gun?" asked Mac.

"Yes, I've seen it in her desk drawer," said Ann. "The only thing that really bothers me about working for Louisa is the number of real nut cases out there. You wouldn't believe the fans who write to her, send her E-mails, gifts with cards saying they love her and want her to put garlic around her windows to keep out alien invaders, stuff like that. There actually was that one about garlic and the aliens. I didn't make it up."

"Anything else about Louisa?" asked Aiden.

"Like?"

"Anything," said Mac.

"She went out every morning for a walk, rain, sun, snow whatever," said Ann, thinking. "When she worked on a book, she sometimes spent the last week or so working away with the door closed and locked."

"You handled her bank account?" asked Mac.

"Accounts, yes."

"Did she ever take large sums out in cash?" asked Aiden.

"Yes," said Ann. "When she finished a book, she would take fifty thousand dollars out of her personal account, in cash."

"What did she do with it?" asked Mac.

"She donated it to her favorite charities," said Ann Chen with a smile. "Put it in envelopes and went herself to slip it under their doors. The NAACP, The Salvation Army, The Red Cross."

"You saw her do this?" asked Aiden.

"No, never. She did it alone, anonymously."

"Did you do her taxes?" asked Mac.

"Yes and no," said Ann. "My brother has an MBA from NYU. He did them with me."

"And," said Aiden, "she declared her donations to charity?"

"No," said Ann. "I urged her to. My brother said it was ridiculous not to, but Louisa insisted that she wasn't using her gifts as a tax dodge. I'm telling you she's a good woman and I can see that you think she might have killed Mr. Lutnikov."

"Did she?" asked Mac.

"No," said Ann. "She was no more likely to do something like that than I am."

"All right," said Aiden. "Did you kill Charles Lutnikov?"

"What? No, why would I? That's really all I have to say. I don't like feeling disloyal to Louisa."

Ann Chen stood up.

"Thank you for the coffee," she said, putting on her coat.

When she was gone, Aiden said, "I'll check with the NAACP and The Salvation Army offices near

Louisa Cormier's building and ask if someone's been slipping envelopes of cash under their doors about the time Louisa comes out with a new book."

"Another coffee?" Mac asked.

"Make it a decaf with half and half, no sugar," she said.

Mac ordered the coffee for her and himself and removed a plastic bag from his kit under the table. He put on his gloves while the young man behind the counter watched perplexed. Mac deposited Ann's used cup in the bag, sealed it, and dropped the bag in his kit.

"You're cops, right?" asked the kid bringing their coffee.

"Yes," said Mac.

"Cool," said the kid.

"How much for the cup?" asked Mac.

"Nothing," said the kid. "No one will notice it's missing. If they do, I'll say a customer broke it."

He looked at Aiden again and said, "You're a cop?"

"I'm a cop," she confirmed.

"You never know, do you," he said and moved back behind the counter as the door opened and a young, laughing couple walked in.

A little over an hour later, Danny sat in the passenger seat of Flack's car while Flack drove. Danny adjusted his glasses and made the call to Stella.

"Hotel manager wants to know who's going to pay for the carpet," he said.

"Tell him to submit a bill to the city," she said.

"I did."

The car came to a stop at a red light and slid to the right, stopping inches away from a small, white delivery truck. The driver looked over at Danny, first with an intake of air expecting a collision and then with a flood of anger.

Even through the frost-covered window Danny could hear the man shouting at them in a language that was definitely Scandinavian. Don Flack calmly removed his wallet from his jacket pocket and reached past Danny to press his badge against the window.

The Scandinavian man, who needed a shave, looked at the badge and flipped his hand to show he didn't care if it was the police, the mayor, the Pope, or Robert DeNiro.

"Video camera on this corner," Flack said, putting his wallet back. "I think somebody should calm the Viking down before he loses it and someone gets hurt."

Danny nodded.

"Danny?" Stella said with exaggerated patience.

"There was nothing in the floor," said Danny. "No holes bigger than ones left by the nails I pulled."

It was what Stella had expected. Danny pushed the button to put Stella on speakerphone so Flack could hear her. Flack had just finished flipping closed his own phone after alerting the video line monitors about the pink-faced Viking who had stepped on the gas as soon as the light had changed. He missed Flack's car by the width of a few sheets of paper and zigzagged forward ahead of them.

"Fingerprint came up with a positive ID," Stella said. "Steven Guista, aka Big Stevie, prior arrests for everything from intimidation to assault and murder. Two convictions for which he served time. One for perjury. One for extortion. Officially, works as a truck driver for Marco's Bakery which is owned by . . ."

". . . Dario Marco," Danny finished.

"Brother of Anthony Marco, who Alberta Spanio was going to testify against tomorrow," she said.

"Mac know?" asked Flack, moving forward, letting the Viking in the van wobble toward the next light.

"I'm going to call him now," she said.

"What do you want me to do?" Danny asked.

"Get back here and become an expert on chains," she said.

"Whips too?" he asked flatly.

She hung up.

Big Stevie sat in Toolie Prine's Bar on 9th Avenue, gargling a cold Sam Adams. Officially, and according to the old-fashioned white letters on the window, the bar was called Terry Malloy's, named after the Marlon Brando character in Big Stevie's favorite movie. Officially, the bar was owned by Toolie's sister, Patricia Rhondov, because Toolie was an ex-con. Officially, Toolie was the bartender. Officially, he still had to report to his parole office once a week. Anybody who knew any of this and most who didn't know any of it still called the place Toolie Prine's.

Big Stevie's behind drooped over the bar stool.

Stevie was strong. It was in his genes. He had never worked out. His old man had been strong, worked on the docks. Stevie could have been a stevedore like his father. He would have been Stevie the Stevedore instead of just Big Stevie.

Toolie's was empty except for Stevie, who liked sitting alone in the amber darkness and looking through the window at cars and people plodding through the snow.

Stevie was pleased with himself. He had done the job he had been told to do. It had been easy—except for the part where he had almost fallen out of the window—and he had ten Benjamin Franklins in his wallet without having to break someone's face or knee. The only drawback was that he had spent four hours listening to the jockey complaining.

Jake the Jockey wasn't a bad guy but he was a complainer. He complained about the picture on the television and the size of the television. He complained about the heat in the room. He complained about the gyros they had eaten which Stevie had thought were particularly good. Stevie had eaten two of them.

The job had gone well, which was why Mr. Marco had given him the day off and the next day—Monday, Stevie's birthday—too. He should do something to celebrate besides coming back and sitting in Toolie's and downing mugs of Sam Adams, but he couldn't think of anything he wanted to do except maybe call Sandrine and have her send a girl, possibly that little Maxine, over to his two-room apartment. He liked small girls. Maybe later if he hadn't had too many beers.

The phone rang and Toolie answered it saying, "Yeah."

Then Toolie handed the phone to Big Stevie, who also said, "Yeah."

Stevie listened carefully.

"Got it," he said and handed the phone back to Toolie.

Big Stevie had another job to do. He wondered if maybe he wasn't getting a little old for this kind of thing.

Tomorrow Big Stevie Guista would be seventy-one years old.

Aiden Burn had called the offices of the NAACP and The Salvation Army. There was no answer at the NAACP, but there was an emergency number.

She called the emergency number and got a woman named Rhoda James, who said that she worked in the office and that she remembered no anonymous donations slipped under the door at any time in the past four years.

There was an answer at The Salvation Army. A Captain Allen Nichols said that he did remember one donation in particular, several years ago, an envelope with a one-hundred-dollar bill found inside the mailbox. As it was just before Christmas, all donations were put into the pot, ranging from a few cents to several thousand dollars. They were all anonymous.

She had passed the information on to Mac before returning to Charles Lutnikov's apartment where she started by taking photographs of all the walls of

Charles Lutnikov's bookshelves. She stood close enough so that the book titles would all show clearly when she blew the photographs up into eight by tens.

She paused at one of the bookcases in the bedroom where two shelves were devoted to pristine copies of what looked to be all the books of Louisa Cormier. Aiden put down her camera and pulled out one of the Cormier books, *Ah, Murder,* from the shelf.

She opened it and went to the title page. It had not been signed by Louisa Cormier. She checked all of the author's books, putting them back after she finished. Her feeling that none of them had been read was confirmed when she flipped through the pages of *Ah, Murder.* Two pages were still attached at the side, had never been sliced or cut, making it impossible for Lutnikov or anyone else to read them. He had not read the books and he had not gotten them autographed by the woman he saw almost every day.

She took out her notebook and wrote a reminder to tell this to Mac. She didn't really need the reminder, but it didn't hurt and it followed procedure.

A random examination of a few dozen of the hundreds of books in the apartment showed that they had been read—jackets showing some wear, spines sometimes split or coming apart, coffee stains and ancient crumbs of toast or doughnut.

And then she turned to the typewriter, lifted the gray metallic top, and leaned forward to examine the black ribbon. Approximately one-third of the ribbon was on the right reel and two-thirds on the left. The ribbon on the right reel was what interested her. She carefully lifted the metal tabs holding each reel and then lifted them out.

Aiden bagged the typewriter ribbon, closed her kit, took a final look around the room, and opened the door. She took one more look back as she ducked under the crime-scene ribbon and closed the door behind her.

Mac sat at the lab station, a pile of slides and photographs of fingerprints taken from the crime scene elevator in front of him.

Mac had great respect for fingerprints, more than for DNA or even confessions. He had made a study of them, had notes in a file cabinet at home on the history of fingerprints, notes he had once planned to turn into a book. He had abandoned that idea the day his wife had died.

Fingerprints simply and truly did not lie. Liars with skill could play tricks with fingerprints, but the fact was simple: There were no two fingerprints alike. A Persian doctor in the fourteenth century had made this discovery. No one had ever found two alike. Even the most uncannily similar identical twins had different fingerprints. Mac had heard a sermon from a police chaplain who suggested that God had included this microscopic truth to show the vastness of his invention. Mac spent little time thinking about that. What interested him was the truth of the statement.

The first use of fingerprints in the United States was in 1882 by Gilbert Thompson of the U.S. Geological Survey in New Mexico. He put his finger-prints on a document to prevent forgery.

A murderer is identified by his fingerprints in Mark Twain's *Life on the Mississippi* in 1883.

The first recorded criminal identification was made in 1892 by Juan Vucetich, an Argentinean po-lice official. He identified a woman named Rojas who had murdered her two sons and cut her own throat to implicate a third party. Vucetich found a bloody fingerprint of Rojas's on a door. The finger-print had been left there before she cut her throat.

In 1897, under the British Council General of India, the first Fingerprint Bureau in Calcutta was established using a classification developed by two Indian experts which is still used today.

Eight years later, in 1905, the United States Army began using fingerprints for personal identification. The Navy and Marine Corps soon followed.

Today the FBI has a computer index, AFIS (Auto-mated Fingerprint Identification System), of more than forty-six million fingerprints of known crimi-nals. Each state also has its own fingerprint file. New York is no exception.

After three hours, Mac concluded that the finger-prints of Ann Chen, Charles Lutnikov, and Louisa Cormier, in addition to many others, were all over the elevator in which Lutnikov had been killed.

Mac wondered when the elevator had last been thoroughly cleaned. He doubted it had been re-cently. He looked at the fingerprints of Lutnikov and the two women. The elevator might be a dead end, but there was still the murder weapon to find and places to look that they might not yet have considered.

Mac sat up, his back aching, and imagined the Rojas woman murdering her children and cutting her own throat. The image was not vivid, but the one of Juan Vucetich finding that fingerprint was.

It was a moment of forensic history that Mac Taylor wished he could have witnessed.

"No problem," the man said, sipping some coffee at the counter in Woo Ching's on Second Avenue uptown.

His egg roll, with two bites out of it, sat in front of him. He wasn't hungry. To his right sat a woman, not old, not young, once pretty, now good looking with short platinum hair. She was lean, well groomed and wore a fur-lined leather jacket and a fur hat. She had taken a few sips of the green tea she had ordered.

It was eleven in the morning on a Sunday, too cold for off-the-street customers except a few seeking respite from the weather over a cup of coffee or tea and a bowl of wonton soup or some egg foo yung.

The only other customers were a trio of women in a booth by the window.

The man didn't know who would be coming to talk to him, only that he was to go to Woo Ching's and have something to eat as soon as he was able to get away. No phones. When she did enter, he had recognized her.

"Details," she said, warming her hands on her

cup, ignoring the small bowl of baked noodles in front of her.

He smiled and shook his head. There was no mirth in his smile.

"What's funny?" she asked.

Neither had looked directly at the other and they wouldn't for the remainder of the conversation. She had come in five minutes after he had ordered, sat across from him and ordered her tea.

"Snow," the man said.

"What's funny about snow?" she asked, checking her watch.

He explained how the snow created a problem they had not anticipated.

"But it's all right?" she asked emphatically.

"It'll be all right," he said, reaching for his pork fried rice, changing his mind and working on the egg roll. "The rest of the money."

"Here," she said removing a thick envelope from her purse and sliding it toward him. He slid the envelope to the edge of the counter, placed it in his jacket pocket, and drank some tea.

She didn't have to tell him what to do if things went badly or a warning call had to be made. He was a pro and he had everything at stake—his life, his family's safety.

She got up, pulled some bills out of her jacket pocket, selected a five dollar bill, dropped it near her cup, and walked toward the door. The man didn't watch her. He waited till he heard the door close before looking around quickly, pretending he was just glancing at the women in the booth and the traffic outside the window. Satisfied that he wasn't being watched, he suddenly felt hungry. He finished his egg rolls quickly, took big bites, savoring the taste even though the egg rolls had gotten just a bit soggy.

Across the street the man in the car with tinted windows had to make a decision, either follow the woman or stay with the man at the counter in the Chinese restaurant. He decided on the woman. He knew where to find the man later.

He flipped down his sun shade, got out of the car, locked it, and went after the woman who was walking slowly, collar turned up, hands in her pockets.

He figured she was heading for the subway station on 86th Street. He was right.

He was also certain that the man she had met in Woo Ching's and to whom she had handed something had something to do with this morning's murder. He meant to find out what it was before people started to pass out more blame, at least some of which would fall on him.

He buttoned his jacket, put on his ear muffs, and followed the woman down the street.

Stella stood over the table looking down at thirty one-foot-long, new metal chains laid out next to the wooden section of window sill that had been removed from the hotel room in which Alberta Spanio had been murdered.

Mac, arms folded, looked down at the display of chains. Danny stood at his side.

"Couldn't be a cable?" Mac asked, pointing at the

groove in the wood and picking up a magnifying glass.

"Take a close look," she said.

It was her turn to fold her arms.

"See it?" she asked.

Mac examined the groove carefully and nodded.

"Cable would leave a smoother groove, neat, cleaner," Stella said. "The groove is half an inch across. All these chains are half an inch."

Mac straightened up and looked at her.

"If the killer came down a half-inch chain to the bathroom below, he or she would have to be really light," Stella said.

"Or really brave," said Danny.

"Or stupid or desperate," said Stella. "And he or she would have to swing through the bathroom window below without disturbing the snow. That, given the size of the space in the open window would mean a supermodel."

"Or a child," said Mac.

Stella shrugged, wondering just how small the man who had been with Stevie Guista when he took the room in the Brevard was.

"Still leaves a big question," she said. "Who was inside the room holding the chain?"

"It wasn't screwed into the floor or tied to any furniture," said Mac, picking up one of the chains.

"No. Danny tore up the floor. No holes. No chain marks or significant scratches in the furniture," she said.

"So, whoever was in the room held the chain."

"Or tied it around himself," Stella added.

"Even so, it would take a strong person to do it,

lower someone down and hold steady while they swung into the bathroom window," he said.

"I tested the strongest chains that would fit marks on the window sill," she said. "Even a ninety pound person on the end of the chain would probably break it, especially if they had to swing through a small space."

"Sounds like a circus act," said Mac.

"Think so?"

"No," he said. "Database. Check for height and weight."

"Can we do that?" asked Danny.

"We can," Mac said.

"Can you see a man or boy dumb enough to let himself be lowered by a chain from a seventh-floor window during a snowstorm?" asked Danny. "Have to be awfully stupid or awfully brave."

"And have a lot of faith in whoever was holding the chain," added Mac.

"And what about that hole in the wood at the bottom of the bathroom window," Stella said. "It's not from a chain. It's from a big screw."

"So," Mac said. "What do we have?"

"A fingerprint belonging to Steven Guista," she said. "Also known as Big Stevie."

"Got an address?"

"He could be out celebrating," she said, handing Mac a fax sheet with Big Stevie's photograph and record on it. "Today's his birthday."

"I wonder what he was celebrating last night," said Mac. "Let's bring him a present."

*　　*　　*

It felt wrong. Flat. Detective Don Flack felt it. No evidence. Gut feeling. He had checked out the door to the bedroom in which Alberta Spanio had been killed. He had asked a maid to go into the room and scream after he closed the door. The maid was Mexican, a legal alien, Rosa Martinez. She didn't want to go into the room where the woman had died hours ago.

"You're not going to lock the door?" she asked.

Even as she asked the question, she knew the answer. The door could only be locked from the inside.

Rosa went in the room, closed the door, and screamed. Then she opened the door.

"Go over by the bed, next to the bed and scream again," he said.

She definitely did not want to go over to the bed in which the woman had died, but she did, and Flack closed the door. She screamed again and then hurried to open the door and step into the outer room.

"OK?" she asked.

"One more thing," Flack said. "Go into the bathroom. Open and close the window and scream."

"Then I'm done?" she asked.

"Then you're done," he said.

Rosa returned to the bedroom, closed the door, moved to the bathroom, and opened the window. Then she screamed once, closed the window, and hurried through the bedroom and into the outer room where the detective was waiting.

"OK," he said. "Thanks."

Rosa left quickly.

The first time she had screamed Flack had heard her, but faintly. The second scream from the bedside was even more faint, and he heard neither the scream from the bathroom nor the opening and closing of the window.

He pulled out his cell phone and called Stella.

They had news for each other.

7

Aiden Burn entered the lab about five minutes after Mac and Stella had departed. She had the lab to herself. The refrigerator in the corner hummed and through the closed glass door she could see only an empty corridor.

She put down her kit, carefully unloaded the contents she needed, placed them next to the microscope, and then went in search of a cup of coffee.

She could get decent coffee from Adelson in firearms but she'd have to politely endure at least five minutes of feeble jokes. She chose the machine instead. With plenty of cream and one of the packets of Stevia in her bag, the coffee was tolerable.

She carried it back to the lab table, carefully placing it several feet from where she was working. No spills. She would move when she wanted a sip.

First she wanted to look at the typewriter ribbon from Lutnikov's apartment, which she did by placing it over a built-in light box in the laboratory table.

She drank some coffee. It was still hot but not burning.

Aiden gently, slowly, rewound the ribbon. It took her a little less than five minutes to get back to the beginning. She laid the ribbon flat and slowly began to wind it again, reading the words that showed through as clear indentations in the black ribbon.

. . . the third door, the last one, the only one left. He, it, had to be behind that door. Peggy had two choices. Run or, fireplace rod in hand, open that last door. It was almost dark, but not quite. Some light came through the window in the hallway of the small house. She had no idea how much light there would be inside the room. She had more than an idea of what she would find, a killer, the person who had brutally dissected three young women and one gay transvestite. The killer would be holding his working tool, a very sharp knife or a scalpel. The killer could be behind the door ready to attack her. Peggy knew she could use the rod. All she had to do was remember the photographs she had been shown of the victims, particularly of her own niece Jennifer. Rod held high in her right hand, Peggy reached for the doorknob. There was still time to turn and run, but if she did that the killer known as The Carver would get away, get away to kill again. There was no point in being quiet. He knew she was in the house, had certainly heard her footsteps on the wooden floor. Peggy turned the knob and shoved the door open.

A hand shot out and caught her wrist as she swung.

"He's dead, Peggy," Ted said releasing her wrist.

His face was bleeding from a cut above his right eye.

She dropped the rod on the floor and fell into his arms.

The End

She looked up, had some more coffee, which was now tepid, and reached for her phone to call Mac. There was still plenty of ribbon to read. Mac picked up the phone after two rings.

"Yes," he said.

She explained what she had found, and he said, "Have it put on a computer and leave it on my desk. I'll pick it up later."

"I'll go to the library," she said.

She hung up.

Stella and Mac got to Steven Guista's apartment just before three o'clock. They had picked up sandwiches at a corner deli and eaten them in the car on the way to Brooklyn. Mac had chicken salad. Stella had egg salad.

"Didn't we have the same thing for lunch yesterday?" she said.

He was driving.

"Yes," he said. "Why?"

"Variety is the spice of life," she said, taking a small bite of her sandwich.

"We get enough variety," he said.

Mac's wife, he remembered, had liked chicken salad, which was probably why he had been eating it. The taste, the smell, reminded him of her. It was something like pinching a taste bud to remind him, though he took no great pleasure in it. He had not been eating well for weeks. Tonight he semi-planned to pick up a couple of kosher hot dogs and a large Diet Coke. The date was coming soon, a few days. As it grew closer, Mac Taylor felt it deeper and deeper inside him. The sky was dark and he sensed more snow coming. He would check the Weather Channel when he got home. He considered calling Arthur Greenberg, then decided against it.

Mac knocked at the door to apartment 4G in the pre-war, three-story brick building. The hallway was dark, but reasonably clean.

There was no answer.

"Steven Guista," Mac said. "Police. Open up."

Nothing.

Mac knocked again. The door across the corridor opened. A lean woman in her fifties stood in the doorway. Her hair was dark and frizzy, and she wore a waitress's uniform with a coat draped over her arm. Next to her stood a girl, very much her mother's daughter, every bit as serious. She couldn't have been more than eleven.

"He's not home," the woman said.

Mac showed his badge and said, "When did you last see him?"

"Yesterday, morning some time," the woman said with a shrug.

"He wasn't home all night," said the girl.

The mother looked at her daughter, making it clear in that look that she wanted to give the police as little information as she could. The girl didn't seem to notice.

"He checks on me at ten," the girl said. "He didn't check last night or this morning."

"I work the evening shift and sometimes nights," the woman said. "Steve is good enough to check on Lilly."

"Sometimes we watch television together," Lilly said. "Sometimes."

"He say something about going to a party or being with relatives or friends today?" Stella asked.

Both girl and woman seemed surprised at the question.

"It's his birthday," said Mac.

"He didn't tell us," the woman said. "I would have gotten him a cake. Maybe I should pick up a present. Steve's been good to us, particularly Lilly."

"He looks scary," said the girl, "but he's very gentle."

"I'm sure he is," said Stella, remembering Stevie Guista's criminal record.

"I've got to go," said the woman, leaning over to kiss her daughter's forehead.

"Lock the door," the woman said.

"I always do," said Lily.

The mother smiled and turned to the two Crime Scene Investigators. "You want us to tell Steve you're looking for him?"

Mac pulled a card from his pocket and handed it to the woman, who handed it to her daughter.

"Did he do something?" asked the girl.

"We just want to talk to him," said Stella.

"About what?" Lilly asked.

Murder, thought Mac, but he said, "He may have witnessed a crime."

"What kind of—?" the girl began, but her mother cut her off.

"Lill, time to go inside. Time for me to go."

The girl said good-bye to Stella and Mac, went inside, and turned the dead bolt.

When the door was closed, the woman said, "I know about his past. Steve is a good man now."

Mac nodded and handed her a second card saying, "Please give this to him when you see him and ask him to give me a call."

The woman took the card, glanced at it, and put it in her coat pocket.

The woman with platinum hair and a fur hat got on a Number 6 subway train at 86th Street with the man following her in the next car. The weather had increased the afternoon crowd, which was fine with the man who could, through the window between cars, see the woman holding onto a steel pole. In spite of her tightly pressed lips, the woman was pretty. The man thought there was something about the way she moved that made him think she was older than she looked, that it was likely her looks had been helped by plastic surgery.

He was a trained, experienced observer and he

was out to save his ass and his job. He would not
lose her. The man had followed her to Woo
Ching's, had seen the woman passing something to
the man next to her. He was too far away to know
what it was. But one thread connected to another,
and now he was following the thread of the
woman. He hoped it would be tied at the other end
to someone else. If he was lucky, that would be the
end of the line. If not, he would have another
thread to follow. He had to keep telling himself to
be patient, though patience had never been one of
his virtues.

When she got off the train at Castle Hill in the
Bronx, he followed her from far enough back that
he was certain he would not be spotted. Now he had
an idea of where she might be headed. He almost
smiled with satisfaction. Almost, but it was too early
to be satisfied.

The woman turned into the entrance of a large,
one-story brick building that half a century had
turned nearly black, with only a smudge of the ancient dirty yellow paint showing through.

When the woman disappeared through the door,
the man moved forward. He knew where she was
going, who she was going to see. He would have to
witness it, tie off the thread.

He went through the wooden doors and found
himself in a dark corridor with doors on both sides.
The satisfying smell of what he was sure was bread
baking filled the air and reminded him of some moment when he was a kid, some holiday, maybe more
than one that smelled like this.

The woman was nowhere in sight. He walked forward, working out his story, feeling the comforting weight of his holstered weapon against his chest under his arm.

Then it happened. No time to go for his gun. No time to do anything except reach up for the arm of the man who had stepped out of the open door of a dark room and circled his thick forearm around the man's throat. When the man reached under his jacket, the big man choking him swatted the hand away and gave a final neck-breaking tug.

The body of Detective Cliff Collier slumped to the floor. The killer looked around and then easily lifted the nearly two hundred pounds of dead weight. He carried the dead man into the darkened office, pushed the door closed, and went to the window.

He opened it and looked around. He really didn't have to look. He knew the alleyway was empty, that only the small truck stood there with open doors.

He dropped the body into a small bank of snow and climbed after it, closing the window behind him. As he lifted the body through the open back doors of the truck, he glanced at the gun in the man's holster, which made him go for the man's wallet.

He was a cop. He hadn't been told he was going to be killing a cop, not that it made any real difference, but for an instant he felt that it would have been right to tell him he was going to be killing a cop.

He closed the truck doors and got into the driver's seat.

Big Stevie had never killed a cop before. No regrets, not really, but it would have been nice if he

had been told. He drove slowly out of the alley, trying to decide where he was going to dump the body.

Mac had left Stella and Don to track down Big Stevie
and went as quickly as weather and traffic would
allow to the upscale apartment building where
Charles Lutnikov had been murdered.

Aiden had called him after sending the typewriter
ribbon back to the lab so the text could be printed by
someone in the NYPD typing pool. She knew a call
from Mac would speed the work but it would still be
a while, perhaps a day or more, till she had a disk
with the contents of the typewriter ribbon on it. Mac
had made the call to the office, assuring the office
manager that the job was urgent.

Aiden was waiting for him in the lobby. He
stamped the snow from his boots before entering
and received a nod of thanks from Aaron McGee,
the doorman.

"People asking lots of questions," McGee said. "I've
got no real answers. What should I tell 'em?"

"As little as possible," said Mac.

"That's what the lady said," McGee said, nodding
at Aiden who stood next to her evidence box. "Not
much I know anyway."

Aiden led the way to the elevator. There was still
a crime-scene tape across the open door. They
ducked under it and Mac looked at Aiden, who said,
"Every inch dusted. Prints of almost everyone in this
part of the building."

Mac pushed the button that would take the elevator up to the penthouse. As the elevator rose, Mac

knelt and examined the thin metal strip at the front of the elevator. There was a small space, perhaps an inch, between elevator rim and the door on each floor. He looked up.

"It's possible," Aiden said, knowing where this was going.

"I'll go with you," Mac said.

They had both seen stranger things than a spent bullet sliding into a small space and getting lost or stuck.

It could be a dirty job.

Aiden hid a sigh and wished for a cup of coffee. The elevator came to a slow gentle stop at the penthouse floor and the doors opened silently.

Mac stepped forward and used the knocker.

Both Aiden and Mac could sense a presence behind the door looking at them through the peephole. The door opened.

"Have you caught him?" asked Louisa Cormier. "The man who shot that poor Mr. Lutnikov?"

"Might have been a woman," said Aiden.

"Of course," said Louisa Cormier with a smile. "I should have said that. Please come in."

She stepped back.

The woman wasn't quite as fashionably chic and casual as she had been earlier. Her hair was almost perfect, but a few of the coiffed curls were slightly out of place and her eyes looked tired. She wore a pair of designer jeans and a white cashmere sweater with the sleeves rolled up revealing a bejeweled watch.

"Please," she said, showing perfect white teeth

and pointing palm up at a small wooden table by the window. There were three chairs around it, all with a panoramic view of the city.

"Coffee? Tea?" she asked.

"Coffee," said Aiden. "Thanks."

"Cream? Sugar?"

"No," said Aiden.

"Cold water," said Mac.

"I let Ann have a few days off," she said as the two police officers sat. "She was really disturbed by the shooting. I'll go get the coffee. I've got a fresh pot started. Frankly, I think she's afraid to come here till the killer is caught. Ann's a gem. I'd hate to lose her."

Louisa Cormier hurried out of the room.

"Anything on the Alberta Spanio killing?" Aiden asked.

"There's always something," Mac said, looking out the window.

Monet had done London, bright and glittering, misty from fog, damp from rain, he thought. Had he ever done New York? What would Monet have seen had he looked out of this window on this day?

Before Louisa Cormier returned, Aiden told Mac that she had re-searched Lutnikov's apartment.

"No sign that he wrote any fiction," she said. "No manuscripts, no sheets in drawers, just what's on the ribbon."

Mac nodded, his mind taking in what he was being told but also wandering out across the rooftops toward the gray skyline.

Louisa Cormier came back with the coffee and a

glass of ice water. She had nothing for herself. When she sat, she ran a hand through her hair.

"Long night," she said. "I have a deadline on a new Pat Fantome novel.

"If you read any of my books, you'll see I'm nothing like Pat unless I'm writing. I leave Pat in my office when I get up from my computer and I become Louisa Cormier everywhere else unless I'm doing a book signing or a talk. Then, I think I let a lot of Pat Fantome take over. I'm grateful to Pat, but she's difficult to live with, driven. I, on the other hand . . ." and she dismissed the rest of the sentence with the wave of her hand.

Aiden sipped the coffee. It was hot, good, exotic. Mac swirled the water in his glass, watching the ice cubes.

"Oh, no," said Louisa Cormier with a laugh at their expressions. "I'm not delusional. There is no Pat Fantome, not really. It's just a mode of thinking I adopt when I write. There are a few similarities between Pat and me, but there are far, far more differences. But you didn't come here to talk about me or Pat. You have questions about poor Mr. Lutnikov."

Mac finally took a drink of water and paused before going on.

"Do you own a gun?" he asked.

Louisa Cormier looked startled and put her right hand to her neck, touching a thin gold band.

"A . . . yes," she said. "A Walther. It's in the office in my desk. You want to see it?"

"Please," said Mac.

"You suspect me of killing Mr. Lutnikov?" she asked, amused.

"We're checking everyone who uses the elevator," said Aiden.

"What more could a mystery writer ask than for material to knock at her door?" said the woman. "I'll get it."

Louisa Cormier, now clearly interested, hurried off toward the closed door to her office.

Mac's phone went off. He answered it, said, "Yes," and listened before saying, "I'll get there as soon as I can. Half an hour."

He hung up as Louisa Cormier came out of the office, gun held by the barrel in one hand. She held out the gun to Mac but he told her to put it on the table.

"I have a permit somewhere," Louisa said. "Ann could find it when . . ."

"I don't think that will be necessary," said Mac.

Aiden put on a fresh pair of gloves and reached for the weapon. Louisa Cormier watched in fascination. After examining the gun, Aiden said, "It's a Walther P22 with a three-quarter-inch barrel. Hasn't been fired recently."

"I don't think it's ever been fired," Louisa said. "It exists in that drawer to satisfy a request from my agent who, I believe, likes me very much, but loves his fifteen percent even more."

"A few questions," said Mac, as Aiden handed the gun back to Louisa Cormier after checking the magazine, which was indeed full. Louisa placed it on the table and sat forward eagerly, clasping her hands on her lap.

"Have you ever been in Charles Lutnikov's apartment?" asked Mac.

"No," said Louisa. "Let me think. No, I don't think so."

"Has he ever been in this apartment?" Mac asked.

"A few times. Actually, whenever a new book of mine comes out, he comes, or should I say came, up rather shyly and asked for an autograph."

"Agent Burn found your books in Mr. Lutnikov's apartment," said Mac. "They were unread."

"That doesn't surprise me," she said. "He was a collector. Signed, unread first editions. He bought another copy to read. He was quite open about that."

"We didn't find any other copies of your books in his apartment," said Aiden.

"He gave them away to other tenants after he read them. After all, he had untouched first editions. My God. This is fascinating."

"Did Lutnikov ever show you any of his writing?" asked Mac.

"His writing? I think he wrote catalogue copy. Why on earth would he show me that?"

"No fiction?" asked Aiden. "Short stories? Poetry?

"No. And to tell the truth, had he done so I would have politely told him I was far too busy to read his work and that I seldom read any fiction, not even that of my closest friends. If he had persisted, as a few do, I would have told him that my agent and editor had told me never to read an unpublished manuscript because I might be accused later of plagiarism. You'd be amazed at how many frivolous lawsuits are filed against me, which is why I contribute significantly to a lobby for tort reform."

"You're working on a book now?" asked Mac.

"Should have it finished in a week or so."

"You work on your computer?" asked Mac.

"I know writers, Dutch Leonard, Loren Estleman, who still use typewriters, but I don't understand why," Louisa said.

"What kind of paper do you use?" asked Aiden.

"In my printer?"

"Yes," said Aiden.

"I really don't know. Something good. Ann gets it at a stationery store on Forty-fourth."

"May we have a sheet of it?" asked Mac.

"A sheet of my computer . . . yes, of course. Is that all?"

"Yes," said Mac. "We're finished for now."

He rose, and so did the two women. Louisa Cormier, gun in her right hand, made another trip to her office and came back with several sheets of paper which she handed to Mac. The gun was gone.

"You should know that I don't give my publisher a printed copy of my books," she said. "Haven't for God knows how many years. I just E-mail the finished manuscript in, and they print it and give it to the copy editor."

"So you have all your manuscripts in files on your computer?" asked Mac.

Louisa Cormier looked at him quizzically.

"Yes, on my hard drive. I also keep a backup floppy disk copy which I lock in my fireproof wall safe."

"Thanks," said Mac. "A last question or two. Do you own another gun?"

Louisa Cormier looked mildly amused.

"No."

"Have you ever fired a gun?"

"Yes, as part of my research. My character Pat Fantome is an ex-police officer with a very good aim. I think it helps to know how it feels to fire a gun. I go to Drietch's Range on Fifty-eighth."

"We'll find it," said Mac. "One more question. Do you have any idea how Lutnikov's blood got on the carpet outside your elevator door?"

"No. I'm really a suspect, aren't I?" She seemed pleased by the possibility.

"Yes," said Mac. "But so are all your neighbors."

"Thanks for the coffee," Aiden said, picking up her kit.

"Come back any time," said Louisa, ushering them to the door. "I'd love to know how your investigation is going. I'm going to call my agent now and tell her about all this."

When they were back in the elevator, Aiden said, "Basement?"

"You're on your own," said Mac. "Stella just found Cliff Collier dead."

"Collier? The cop who was guarding Alberta Spanio?"

"Strangled."

"Where?"

"Alley in Chinatown."

Aiden nodded and stifled a sigh with a stiff-lipped nod. She would have to go in search of the bullets by herself. She had been at the bottom of elevator shafts before. It was always interesting. It was never pleasant.

Mac looked at the sheets of paper in his hand.

He and Aiden were both thinking the same thing.

"Search warrant?" she asked.

He shook his head.

Louisa Cormier had lied. Both Aiden and Mac knew it, but they didn't know what she had lied about—probably the blood traces. It was a rare suspect who didn't lie about something, even if they were completely innocent.

"Not enough cause," he said.

"We can ask her nicely," Aiden said.

"And she can say 'no' nicely and call her lawyer."

"So?"

"We'll find more evidence," he said.

8

"DONE?" ASKED THE MAN.

"Done," answered Big Stevie Guista.

Big Stevie had made the phone call from a bar down the street from Zabar's. He had a shopping bag full of food—sausages, rolls, cheeses—a large slice of Gorgonzola, his favorite-flavored spreads, soft drinks, and powdered sugar cookies.

His plan was to have a mini-birthday party with Lilly, the little girl who lived across the hall from him. Her mother would be at work.

If Big Stevie had ever gotten married and had ever had kids, his grandchildren would be Lilly's age. Maybe. She was a good kid. He'd party with her, maybe watch a little television. Tomorrow he'd get laid. Happy Birthday Steven Guista. He wasn't complaining.

"Good," the voice on the other end said.

Both the man and Stevie knew better than to say any more. They hung up.

Stevie's delivery truck was parked illegally in front of a fire hydrant that was just barely sticking its top through a mound of snow. There was no ticket under the wiper when he got in. There never was. The police, the other people who saw the parked truck, usually thought he was making a delivery, which was what he would claim if someone confronted him. There weren't many people willing to confront Big Stevie about anything.

Stevie backed out of the parking space carefully, looking back over his shoulder, which was difficult to do because he had very little in the way of a neck.

The back of his small truck was empty, the wire racks clear. He had delivered the body of the cop to the alleyway more than two hours earlier. There was no smell of death, only the familiar diminishing scent of once-fresh bread.

Stevie liked that smell. He liked it better when the bread was fresh. All in all Stevie liked his work.

The body lay behind a Dumpster in an alley behind Ming Lo's Dim Sum in Chinatown. What had once been Cliff Collier lay on his back, feet straight out, arms roughly folded across his chest, head at an odd angle as if he had been looking almost behind him.

Stella had eaten at Ming Lo's at least a dozen times, always on Sunday mornings, always with some relative who came to New York wanting to see something of the city. Ming Lo's entrance, which was on the other side of the building on Mott Street, was brightly neon lit with a broad escalator inside the glass doors. At the top of the escalator was a massive room jammed with tables. Chinese men and women wheeled dim sum carts around for customers, almost all Chinese, who selected from dozens of choices, all of which were eaten with chop sticks or fingers. Stella's relatives were always impressed.

She wondered how impressed they would be by the sight of the dead man in the alley.

"This is what I do," she said, imagining a conversation with an aunt or cousin. "I ask dead people questions."

The idea of dim sum, which usually made her hungry, now made her feel slightly nauseated. Her stomach was churning. Stella knelt next to the body. Danny had already taken photographs of the dead man, the wall, and the Dumpster.

Don Flack was near the rear door of Ming Lo's talking to the kitchen worker who had discovered the body. The clearly frightened heavy-set man responded in Chinese, which was translated by a young woman in a silk dress who shivered as she spoke.

Flack took off his coat and wrapped it around the young woman's shoulders. She nodded her thanks. The heavy-set man spoke rapidly, excited.

"He knew the dead man wasn't homeless," the young woman translated. "He is dressed too well and his hair is cut."

Flack nodded, notebook in hand.

"Did he see anyone, hear anything?" Flack asked.

The young woman translated. The heavy-set man shook his head emphatically.

Flack looked back at the body. He had known Collier, not well but well enough to use first names and feel comfortable about asking each other about their families. Don remembered that Collier wasn't married but had a mother and father who lived in Queens. Collier's father was a retired cop.

Danny, Stella, and Don all noticed the smell, a mixture of warm, salty and sweet Chinese cooking. Danny would have liked an order of fried wonton or something else that looked good. Maybe he could suggest to Stella that when they finished outside they might go inside, ask some questions, get something to eat.

Stella gently touched the neck of the dead man and turned the body slightly. It was tight behind the Dumpster but she managed to reach back for her small hand vacuum and use it on the victim's jacket, neck, and hair.

Flack wasn't thinking of Chinese food. Not that he didn't like it, but the dead man was on his mind and he was focused.

"Thanks," he said to the young woman.

She didn't have to translate. The heavy-set man glanced at the body and hurried back into the restaurant. The girl handed Flack's coat back to him. Their eyes met. There might have been something there, but he wasn't up to it, not now, not here, not with Collier lying there.

When the girl went back in the restaurant, Flack turned and watched Mac Taylor coming down the alley, moving slowly, hands deep in the pockets of his coat.

Mac stood next to Danny, looking down at the

body and Stella kneeling next to it. Mac's lips were closed and tight, his eyes searching the narrow alley.

"Neck's broken," Stella said.

She turned the body on its side. It was a tight fit and the dead man was heavy. She could have asked for help, but she didn't want to contaminate the site any more than it had been already.

"Alley's full of prints in the snow," said Danny. "At least six different people. I've taken footprints."

Danny had first used an aerosol spray snow print wax to retain the details of the prints and stop the effects of melting. Then he had taken a casting of each print, using a pouch of casting powder mixed with water, which he kneaded and poured directly from the pouch into the print, adding a couple of pinches of salt to speed the setting of the plaster.

"Any particularly large?" asked Mac.

"One set," said Danny. "Clean one over here."

Danny knew why Mac had asked about large prints. Collier was over six feet tall and more than two hundred pounds. He was also in good shape, worked out. Hawkes would weigh him to get an exact figure.

Whoever had killed Collier had been stronger and at least as big as the detective, if it was one killer. Again, Hawkes would be able to tell them more.

Danny pointed to a trio of footprints heading toward the Dumpster and then at two more, approximately the same size, heading away. The ones heading away weren't as deep as the ones heading toward the Dumpster. The weight of Collier's body had been off of the shoulders of the man who had dropped the body.

"Get a cast of the footprints moving away," said Mac. "Measure the snow density. We'll find a formula to be sure that he was carrying Collier's body. Check Collier's wallet. See what it gives as his weight."

Danny nodded. There was no doubt that the footprints belonged to the bearer of Collier's body, but it might come down to evidence given in court and Mac wanted everything confirmed.

Flack joined Danny and Mac and watched Stella work.

The question didn't have to be asked, but all four members of the CSI unit knew the odds of the detective's murder being connected somehow to the murder of Alberta Spanio, the woman he had been protecting only hours ago.

Stella was up now, taking off her gloves.

Mac could see the places on the Dumpster that had been dusted for prints. There were plenty of them, but it wasn't likely that any belonged to whoever had dropped Collier's body here.

"He wasn't killed here," Stella said.

Mac nodded.

"No footprints in the snow behind the body," she said. "If he was killed and pushed over, he'd have to be turned around. No sign of that."

"No signs of struggle," said Mac.

"That too," said Stella.

"We've got footprints," said Danny.

It was Stella's turn to nod. There was nothing more for them to do here. The rest would be done in the lab.

Each of them had a theory, one they were ready to give up or modify with the next piece of evidence.

Flack's first thought was that Collier had found a lead to Alberta Spanio's murderer, followed it and got spotted by the killer.

Danny considered that Collier may have seen or remembered something about the murder and either told the wrong person, or the killer figured out that Collier knew something that might reveal who he was.

Stella considered that Collier might have been involved in the murder of Alberta Spanio and had been killed to protect the killer or killers.

"Ed Taxx," Mac said. "Bring him in. He may be on the killer's list. If Collier saw or knew something that got him killed, Taxx might know the same thing."

Flack nodded.

"And let's find Stevie Guista," Mac added, glancing at the body and nodding at the paramedics who had just arrived.

Mac checked his watch.

"Anyone hungry?" he asked.

"Yeah," said Danny, rubbing his hands together and shifting his feet which were beginning to feel numb.

"I'll pass," said Stella.

Don shook his head and watched the paramedics move the Dumpster and zip the dead man into a black bag.

The quartet didn't move. They watched silently until the body was well down the alley. Mac noticed a trio of wrapped fortune cookies lying in the snow where the Dumpster had been. He knelt and picked them up.

Mac and his wife had been to Ming Lo's once. They'd had fortune cookies that night. He didn't remember what they said.

After a few seconds, he dropped the unopened fortune cookies in the Dumpster and turned to the others, saying, "Dim sum?"

Big Stevie knocked at the door and waited while Lilly said, "Who is it?"

"Me, Stevie," he said.

When she opened the door, he handed her the shopping bag from Zabar's. It weighed her down and touched the floor.

"It's my birthday," he said. "How about a birthday party?"

He stepped in and closed the door behind him.

"I knew it was your birthday," she said, moving to the small kitchen and starting to lift out each of the goodies, pausing to savor the touch and smell of what was to come. "I made you a present."

Stevie was caught off guard, touched. It must have shown on his face.

"It's nothing much," Lilly said. "I'll give it to you after we eat."

He took off his coat and removed his shoes, placing the coat on the chair near the door and the shoes on a mat next to the chair.

"How about before we eat," he said, trying to remember the last time he had been given a birthday present. Not since he was a young boy. He had never been a "little" boy.

"Okay," Lilly said, removing the last package from the shopping bag.

She moved to the bedroom on the left, went in, and came back seconds later with a small package awkwardly wrapped in wrinkled red paper with a pink ribbon. She placed the small package in his huge hand.

"Open it," she said.

He did, carefully, not tearing paper or ribbon. It was a small, pocket-sized animal. Lilly had made it from clay or something and painted it white.

"It's a dog," she said. "I was going to make a horse but it was too hard. You like it?"

"Yes," he said, putting the dog on the table.

It wobbled but didn't fall.

"Can I name him?" Lilly asked.

"Sure."

"Rolf, like the dog on *Sesame Street*."

"Rolf," he said. "Sounds like a bark."

"I think it's supposed to."

"So," he said. "Should we eat?"

Lilly got plates, knives, forks, paper towels, and glasses.

"Did those people find you?" she, asked unwrapping a package of sausage.

"People?" Stevie asked.

"A man and a woman, when Mom left for work."

"Who did they say they were?" he asked as Lilly

carefully placed a slice of sausage on a roll she cut in half.

"I think they were the police," she said, handing him the sandwich she had made and then the card her mother had given her before she left.

Stevie was silent. He looked at the CSI card with Mac Taylor's name and number on it and handed it back to the girl. Then he took the sandwich and looked at it as if it were an unfamiliar object.

"I think one of them is in your apartment waiting for you," she said, working on her own sandwich.

Stevie pocketed the clay dog and turned in his chair to look at the door as if he could, with enough effort, see through it into his own apartment.

Stevie had to think. It would take time. Thinking was not one of his strong points. He took a large bite of the dry sandwich. The texture was dry, but the taste was satisfying, familiar.

Jacob Laudano was seriously starting to worry. It had all been too easy, and now he had a phone call telling him what to say if and when the police came looking for him.

Why the hell should the police be looking for him? Okay, so they had a reason to look for him, but he could get around that unless they were out to nail him. They didn't have evidence against him. They couldn't.

Jacob "The Jockey" Laudano stood four foot ten and weighed ninety-four pounds, five pounds more than his racing weight. Considering that the last time he had been on a horse was eight years ago, he had done a good job of keeping the weight off, putting food on the table, paying the rent for his one-bedroom East Side apartment, and having enough left over for clothes and drinks.

He didn't need money to get women, not like Big Stevie. Not many wanted to be crushed by Steve's bulk or look up and see Steve's face. Jake, on the other hand, held an appeal for some reason that was hard for him to understand, but which he accepted without question. He knew it had something to do with his size. He wasn't a bad looking guy, but the face that looked back at him in the morning mirror or the mirror at the back of Denny Kahn's Bar was no Tom Cruise. Jake was pale, nose a little sharp, eyes narrow. He was nearing fifty but could pass for younger. His size again.

He had never liked the horses except to bet, and that's what had gotten him into trouble. For awhile it had been good. He had bet on his own races and played all the tricks to see to it that the favorite didn't win. It was a little-appreciated skill, even less appreciated by the other jockeys who eventually turned him in.

Jake was through in the business by the time he was twenty-six, at which time he had put his agility and lack of regard for the law into the traditional family business, breaking and entering.

He had done fine at that for more then ten years and then, dumb luck, he was delving into the lower drawer of a dresser where people often hid something small and worth taking when the apartment door opened suddenly.

Dumb luck. Jake had gone for the window. The guy had beat him to it, blocked his way, and punched him in the chest harder than he had ever been punched before or than he would be while doing two years upstate.

The guy turned out to be a third baseman for the Mets. Dumb luck again.

Jake made contacts while on the inside, which led to connections when he got out, connections that got him work because he was still damned good at getting in and out of places the big, fat, and often old people who hired him could not fit into. The first time he had been offered a hit for ten thousand he had said, "Sure."

He had killed three others since then, all for the standard fee of $10,000. Jake the Jockey had a reputation. He didn't try to hold out for a bigger payoff no matter who he was hired to kill.

Jake's preferred tool was a long, sharp knife to the neck while the mark was asleep.

He was straightening his tie in the mirror and pulling the knot just right. Someone had once called him a "natty dresser." He had looked it up and liked it.

The phone rang. Jake kept working on his tie as he came out of the bathroom and picked it up.

"Yeah," he said.

And then he listened.

"Went just fine," Jake said. "Like I told you. In, out. No questions . . . Yeah, they saw me, not my face. . . . If he does, I will, but he won't come here . . . Okay, okay, I'll call."

The phone went dead. He put it back down and looked at it for a few seconds. Had something gone wrong?

It was dark in the elevator shaft, but Aiden had a large lamp flashlight on its highest setting sitting in a corner on a metal beam.

She wore gloves and had a package of evidence bags atop her kit next to the flashlight. There wasn't as much garbage as she had expected, but there was still enough to make the job formidable.

It was a challenge.

There were crumbling sheets from newspapers dating back to the 1950s. One of them held the word "Ike" in what was left of the headline. She plowed through envelopes, all old, none from or to anyone whose name she recognized. She found a Baby Ruth candy bar wrapper, an assortment of screws, thumb tacks, and other pieces of metal. She found two dead rats under an unidentifiable moist mess in one corner. One of the rats was long dead and mostly skeletal. The other was still damp and all too fragrant.

She rummaged for forty-five minutes, finishing her search with a dried out condom wrapped in aluminum foil. So much for a high-class Manhattan apartment building.

There was no bullet at the bottom of the shaft. She was as sure of that as the fact that she needed a shower.

She started to climb out of the shaft into the basement. With one knee on the concrete floor, she took a last look back, shining her flashlight into corners

and up at the stopped elevator, which she'd turned
off before coming down here. It was then that she
saw it. The bullet, what was left of it, lay dark and
leaden, on a metal structural beam. It hadn't fallen
all the way to the floor of the shaft.

Aiden scrambled down into the shaft with tweez-
ers and a plastic bag, took three photographs, and retrieved the bullet.

9

HAWKES LOOKED DOWN AT COLLIER'S BODY, Mac and Stella at his side.

"The killer was taller than the victim," Hawkes said. "Look at the bruises."

He pointed to the dead man's neck.

"Pulled back and up to get leverage. Bruises start at the Adam's apple and work upwards. Like this."

Hawkes got behind Mac and demonstrated. Mac could feel Hawkes's loose grip moving upward.

"Probably lifted our victim right off the ground."

Hawkes stepped back and looked down at the corpse again.

"Dead man weighs two hundred and ten pounds and is six one and a half," Hawkes said. "Your killer is at least six five, maybe as tall as six six or even six seven and very strong. No fumbling around here, just one clean arm around the neck from behind and a powerful sudden pull. No struggle."

"And?" asked Stella.

"Killer's right-handed," said Hawkes. "Principal

bruising and crushing of the esophagus is on the victim's right side."

"So if we find a left-handed giant, he's innocent?" asked Mac straight faced.

"Thus eliminating left-handed giants," Hawkes agreed.

"He's done this before," said Stella.

"He knew what he was doing," said Hawkes. "You like opera?"

"Never saw one," said Stella.

Mac had seen them. His wife had loved opera. And Mac had gotten used to the artificial, inane stories, the overacting, and the semi-pomp of dressing up. He had especially liked watching Claire dress for a big night out. She always smiled in anticipation. And Mac had gradually grown to appreciate the music and the singing.

"I've got two tickets for *Don Giovanni* tomorrow," Hawkes said. "Donatelli in Homicide gave them to me. He's got a cousin in the chorus. Donatelli's wife has the flu, which, he said, was one he owed God."

"You're not going?" asked Stella.

"I prefer CDs," said Hawkes. "You want to try?"

"No, thanks," said Stella.

"Mac?" asked Hawkes.

Mac considered and looked at Stella.

Her cheeks were pink, but it was difficult to tell how pink under the surgical lights. Her eyes were moist and he thought she looked a little unsteady.

"Take them," she said.

"You all right?" he asked.

"A cold," she said.

Mac held out his hand and Hawkes produced two tickets from his pocket. Mac glanced at them. They were good seats, orchestra.

"Thanks," he said, pocketing them.

On the way down the corridor, with gray frigid light coming through the windows, Stella asked, "You really like opera?"

He almost said, "We did," but stopped himself and instead said, "Depends on the opera."

In the lab, Danny Messer stood in front of a large table on which lay a two-foot length of steel chain.

"Where do we start?" he said, looking at Stella and Mac.

Mac jerked his chin at the chain.

"Right," said Danny. "Standard stuff. Some of the links have tiny numbers indicating their manufacturer. One thing's for sure. This chain matches the fragments we got in that hotel room. I called the manufacturer. They guarantee the chain will hold a hundred pounds. The woman I talked to said that holding more than a hundred pounds on the chain out the window would probably result in one or more of the links opening."

"Collier's clothes?" asked Mac.

Danny smiled and walked over to a microscope. Alongside the microscope were slides neatly numbered. Danny put one of the slides in the microscope, focused, and stepped back.

"Tested the brown-white flecks," Danny said. "Flour. On the back of his jacket only."

Stella examined the slide.

"Collier's body was moved in a vehicle containing flour," said Mac.

"Almost coated in a thin layer," said Danny.

"Insect pieces in the flour," Stella said. "In the other samples too?"

"Yep," said Danny.

"Federal Drug Administration allows a low level of insect content in flour used in bakeries," said Mac.

"I'll remember that when I order a sub for dinner tonight," said Danny.

Stella moved aside and Mac gazed into the microscope saying, "Insects are different for each bakery."

"And," added Danny, "there are different kinds of flour, different additives. I'm tracing the producer of this flour. I'll get a list of their customers. Then we can match the flour and insect particles to a particular bakery."

"Maybe," said Stella, arms folded.

"Maybe," Danny agreed.

"Start with Marco's Bakery," said Stella.

They all knew why. The fingerprint in the hotel room above Alberta Spanio's bedroom had been left by Steven Guista, a man with an arrest record, a big man who drove a truck for Marco's Bakery, which was owned by Dario Marco, the brother of the man Alberta Spanio was supposed to testify against.

"Nothing from Flack?" asked Mac.

"Nothing yet," said Danny. "He's waiting at Guista's apartment. Judge Familia issued the warrant."

Mac looked at Stella, who held back a sniffle.

"I'll get my kit," she said.

It would take them twenty minutes to get to
Guista's apartment. A lot would happen in those
twenty minutes.

Don Flack carefully examined Guista's small apartment, listening for footsteps in the hall. A monk
could have lived there.

There was a stained green recliner in the small
living room just inside the door to the hall. The
stained recliner had a hollowed-out indentation
where Guista probably spent most of his time. A
small color Zenith television sat on top of an old
three-drawer dresser directly in front of the recliner.
A remote sat on the arm of the recliner.

There was a Formica-covered table in the kitchen
with aluminum legs and three matching chairs with
blue plastic seats and backs. A refrigerator with little
in it, a cupboard with three coffee cups, four dinner
plates, a pair of heavy glasses. Under the sink were
one pot and one chipped Teflon-covered pan.

The bedroom was tiny. A big neatly made bed
with a green blanket and four pillows took up most
of the bedroom space. There were no books or magazines on the night table. On the wall at the foot of
the bed was a print of three horses eating grass in a
broad rolling pasture.

The small bathroom had an oversized old tub
with clawed feet and old porcelain handles.

What struck Flack most about the apartment was
that it appeared to be immaculately clean, almost
antiseptic, barely lived in. There weren't many
clothes in the drawers or closet. Guista did seem par-

tial to green in his socks, shirts, and few pieces of furniture.

Don went back in the living room/kitchen area and sat in one of the chairs at the Formica-covered table. The chair faced the door.

Don was prepared to spend the rest of the day and all night in the small apartment.

Across the hall, Big Stevie and Lilly partied, ate, and began to watch a rerun of a *Gunsmoke* episode, one of the ones in black and white with Dennis Weaver as Chester.

Stevie wanted to stay there. He had done enough for one day, more than enough. He hoped it would be appreciated. He didn't expect a bonus. A small sign of appreciation would do. And it was his birthday.

But right now he had to think. There was someone in his apartment, a man, waiting for him, going through his neatly stacked clothing, his evenly spaced pants, shirts, and jackets, his coffee cups and cereal jars.

Big Stevie knew he had to get away, but it felt right sitting with Lilly, eating the last of the cake, drinking orange-tangerine juice.

It was most likely the cops. But it was too soon for them to find him. In fact, he did not expect to be found at all, but here they were.

Then another thought welled up. He tried to push it down. What if it wasn't the cops? What if Mr. Marco thought Big Stevie might get picked up, might talk? What if Mr. Marco thought Big Stevie was getting too old for the work? No, couldn't be. Wouldn't happen. But maybe.

Stevie had to get into his apartment, find out. He had to get the few things he cared about in there and go somewhere, check in with Marco and go to Detroit or Boston. He knew Detroit and Boston.

"I'm not afraid," Lilly said.

"What?"

"That man inside the barn isn't going to kill Marshall Dillon," she explained. "The music says he might, but if he killed Marshall Dillon, there'd be no more shows and we know there were lots of them."

"You're smart," said Stevie, touching the top of her head with a broad palm.

"Smarter than the average bear," she said.

Stevie didn't get it.

The show ended. Marshall Dillon shot the bad guy in the barn. Stevie stood up. He had to know.

"You stay in here," he said. "You might hear some noise in the hall but you stay in here. Lock the door behind me."

"You have to go?"

"Business," he said.

"The man in your apartment," said Lilly.

"Yeah."

"Are you coming back when you're finished with him?"

"Not today," he said.

He put his hand in his pocket and pulled out the painted dog she had made for him.

"Thanks," he said, holding it up.

"You really like it?"

"Best birthday present I ever got," he said, putting the dog back in his pocket.

He turned down the volume on the television set, walked to the door, opened it slowly, quietly, while Lilly watched.

"Lock it," he whispered.

She nodded, followed him to the door, and locked it behind him.

In the hall, Stevie stood still for a few seconds and then moved silently to his apartment door. Did the man inside leave the door unlocked? Probably not. He would want to hear Stevie put his key in the lock, turn it, which was why Stevie instead threw himself at the door.

Don should have been ready, but the huge man who flew past the splintered door and lunged at him was moving too quickly for the detective to pull out his weapon.

He started to rise from the chair but the big man flung himself toward him, landing with his full weight on Don, sending them both toppling to the floor.

"Police," Don panted.

The big man was on top of the detective who was pinned to the floor, pain in his back from the metal leg of the chair digging into it.

Stevie was relieved. Marco had not sent someone to kill him. Stevie could deal with the police. He had his entire life. Anthony Korncoff, who had spent half his life in cells, said Stevie's survival was a direct result of Stevie's relative lack of intelligence.

"You're all animal instinct," Korncoff had said.

Stevie had taken it as a compliment. Stevie kept everything simple. He had to. Once Stevie told a lie, he stuck to it. He couldn't be, had never been rattled. He wasn't rattled now.

"What do you want?" said Stevie.

"Get off me and we'll go in for a few questions," said Don, trying to ignore the pain and the weight of the big man.

"Questions about what?" asked Stevie.

It was possible this man pinning Don to the floor had murdered Cliff Collier a few hours earlier. It was certain he had something to do with Alberta Spanio's murder. It was likely that if Don said any of this, the big man would kill him.

"Let me get some air," Don gasped.

Stevie considered and sat back. It was a mistake. Don got to his gun and was pulling it out of the holster under his jacket when Stevie's fingers found his throat.

Don could feel the thick thumbs digging into his neck, deeply, quickly. He fired. He wasn't sure where the gun was aiming. He hoped it was toward Big Stevie Guista.

Stevie grunted, his thumbs loosened slightly. Don hit the big man in the nose with the barrel of his gun and Stevie stood up on wobbly legs, blood coming from a wound in the fleshy upper part of his left leg, blood flowing from his broken nose.

Don skittered backwards on the floor. He still wanted to take the man in, but he wasn't going to take any chances.

He hesitated. Big Stevie kicked the gun out of the

detective's hand. The gun rose and landed with a clatter in the kitchen sink.

Stevie had a choice. There had been a shot. People might have heard. Should he kill the policeman? Did he have enough strength to do it? Would it make the pain and bleeding worse? And what was there to gain from killing another cop?

There was no choice. Stevie lumbered past the open door and into the hall.

Behind him he could hear the cop trying to get up. The door to the apartment across from his opened. Lilly stood there looking at him.

"I'll be all right," he said. "Go back in. Lock your door."

"You're hurt," she said plaintively, seeing the wound in his leg.

She began to cry.

He glanced back at the cop who was struggling to get up.

"No one ever cried for me before," he said.

He smiled through the blood that covered his face and turned his teeth red.

Stevie staggered quickly down the hall without looking back. His hand found the painted dog in his pocket. He held it tightly, but not so tightly that it would break.

Mac and Stella missed Stevie by no more than three minutes. They saw the drops of blood on the stairway as they climbed the stairs. They didn't know whose blood it was but they could tell that whoever had been bleeding had gone down the stairs, not up.

The blood drops left a small tail in the direction from which the bleeding person had come.

When they stood in the doorway of Stevie's apartment, Mac had his gun drawn.

The little girl from across the hall who they had talked to earlier was kneeling next to Don Flack, who sat on the floor, wincing.

"Rib or two broken I think," he said. "Guista can't be far. Couple of minutes ago. Shot him."

Stella moved to Don's side as Mac turned, gun in hand, and followed the trail of blood.

The woman, tall, pretty, short platinum hair, probably somewhere in her mid-forties, wore a gray suit, white blouse, and a simple strand of faux pearls around her neck. She exuded class amid the smells of baking bread. The faint sound of voices wafted from the bakery down the hall and beyond the double doors.

Danny wanted to adjust his glasses but kept from doing it. Somehow he thought the woman would pick up on the move as insecurity.

"You want to see Mr. Marco about . . . ?" she asked, looking at the uniformed officer behind Danny. The officer was broad, experienced, dark-skinned. His name was Tom Martin. He met the woman's eyes without blinking.

One of the first lessons he had learned twenty-one years ago in the Academy was that when you were faced with a tough nut, don't blink. Literally, figuratively, don't blink. His instructor, a much-decorated veteran, had suggested that they watch the eyes of movie stars.

"Charlton Heston, Charles Bronson," the instructor had said. "They don't blink. That's part of their secret. Make it part of yours."

Martin knew where they were and why. No trouble was expected, but he had gone through seemingly innocent doors before and found himself facing semi-human or stone-cold madness. That was how he had earned the pink scar on his chin and a lot of experience.

"Mr. Marco is busy," said the woman, who didn't introduce herself.

"I just want to look in the bakery and ask a few questions," Danny said.

"I can answer your questions," she said.

"Is Steven Guista here?"

"He has today and tomorrow off," she said. "His birthday. Mr. Marco remembers the birthdays of those loyal to him."

Danny nodded.

"Is his truck here?" asked Danny.

"No," she said. "Mr. Marco let him use it for transportation for his birthday."

"A truck?" asked Danny.

"A small delivery truck," she said.

"I'd like to see the bakery and Mr. Marco now," Danny said. "I could come back with a warrant."

"I'm sorry, but . . ." she began.

"You sell your bread?"

"That's what we're in business to do," she said.

"I'd like to buy a fresh loaf," Danny said.

She turned her head slightly trying to decide if he was trying to be funny.

"What kind?" she asked.

"Whatever kind Guista delivers," Danny said.

"We have eight different kinds of bread," she said.

"One of each," said Danny. "I'll pay retail."

"Wait here," she said and moved quickly down the corridor toward the bakery doors, her flat heels clicking on the well-worn tile.

The office door was to the left of the two men. Dario Marco's name was on it in gold letters. Danny looked at Martin, who nodded and opened the door. The two men walked in and found themselves in a small wood-paneled reception area/office. On the desk was a name plate: Helen Grandfield.

Behind the desk was a door. From behind the door came the voice of man. Danny and Martin moved to the door. Danny knocked and went in without waiting for a reply.

Dario Marco, lean, wearing slacks and a white shirt open at the collar, stood in front of his desk talking on the phone. They had interrupted his pacing. He stopped suddenly, looked at the two men, and said, "I'll call you back."

He hung up the phone and turned to face Danny and Martin.

"I don't remember saying 'come in,' " he said.

He was in his early sixties, hair obviously dyed. He had probably been darkly good looking as a young man, but the weight of whatever he had done with his life wore heavily on his sagging features.

"Sorry," said Danny.

"What do you want?"

"When did you last talk to your brother?" asked Danny.

Marco looked at the beat cop, whose eyes met his. Martin won. He was better trained. Marco blinked and turned back to Danny, indicating by looking the CSI investigator up and down that he wasn't impressed.

"Which one?" asked Marco.

"Anthony."

Marco shook his head.

"Anthony's the black sheep in the family," Dario Marco said. "We don't talk. I haven't even visited him in prison."

The look he gave Danny was a challenge. There were lots of ways to communicate with someone in prison.

"Check his phone calls, the visitors log," said Dario.

"We did," said Danny.

"So what else you want?"

"Steven Guista," said Danny.

"He's off. His birthday. I gave him two days. Had to lay off seven bakers and cut production in half since this low carb shit started. Bread's the bad guy now. You imagine? Staff of life. Right in the Bible for Christ's sake. What do you want with Stevie? He done something?"

"We'd like to talk to him and take a look at his delivery truck," said Danny.

"He's driving it."

"I know. Your secretary told us," said Danny.

"Helen's my assistant," he said.

The door opened and the woman came in with a large white paper bag.

"I'm sorry," she said to Marco.

She didn't sound sorry. Marco shrugged it off. She handed the bag to Danny.

"If you don't mind, I'd like to go to the bakery and pick out my own bread," said Danny.

"You think I ran out and bought bread on the street?" she asked.

Danny shrugged and couldn't resist the urge to adjust his glasses.

"It's okay," said Marco. "Show the gentlemen the bakery and then show them the door."

Turning to Danny he added, "No more questions. You come back, you come with a warrant."

Helen Grandfield turned and led the two men out the door. They followed her down the corridor and through the doors to the bakery. The smell of baking bread was strong, good and comforting.

"Take what you like," Helen said as about a dozen bakers and bakers' assistants in white aprons and white disposable paper hats glanced at them and kept working.

Danny collected rolls and bread in another white paper bag, then placed both bags on the floor while he scooped up flour from a table where cords of un-baked loaves sat waiting for the oven. He dropped the flour into another bag.

"Thanks," Danny said, handing his evidence kit to Martin and picking up the two paper bags.

Martin noticed that the CSI officer held the bags

with his fingers across the top. Danny Messer was preserving Helen Grandfield's fingerprints.

"That's it?" she asked.

"That's it," Danny agreed.

He moved to the bakery door with Martin at his side. Helen Grandfield didn't follow them. On the way out, Danny automatically scanned the walls, the floor, listened, smelled. They were a few dozen feet down the corridor past Marco's office in front of another dark office door when Danny stopped and looked down. Martin followed his eyes and watched as Danny went to one knee.

There were two dark lines about a foot long and about six inches apart. Opening his kit, Danny took photographs of the marks and then carefully took scrapings of the material of which the smudges were made.

When he was almost finished, the bakery door at the far end of the corridor opened. Danny and Martin looked back at Helen Grandfield.

Her eyes met Danny's across the distance. He didn't mind being the first to blink. His mind wasn't on outstaring the cat. It was about dark smudges that might, just might, from their color, touch, and smell, be heel marks.

10

MAC HIT THE STREET IN TIME to see the small white truck with MARCO'S BAKERY printed on the back pull out of a loading zone in front of a deli.

He hurried, almost slipped on the ice under the layer of snow, and got to the loading zone in time to see the white truck make a wobbly right turn at the corner about a hundred feet away.

Stella was at his side now. Neither of them were panting but the cold air bit into their lungs. They both knew that by the time they got back to their car and gave chase, Guista would be gone.

Mac looked down at the street about where the driver's side entrance of Guista's car would have been. The splotch of blood was about the size of the top of a Pepsi can. Guista was bleeding more now. His run to the truck had made his wound worse.

Stella had a small kit in her pocket. She knelt next to the splotch of blood, took out a swab, collected and bottled a blood sample. She did the same with a second swab and bottle and then put the samples back into the kit and her pocket.

A few people walking by paused to watch, but only for a few seconds. It was just too damned cold.

"Now?" Stella said, getting up, trying not to show the ache in her arms and legs.

"We call hospitals," Mac said as a car with illegal snow chains rattled past them. "We call for a lookout on the truck."

"He's bleeding badly, deep," Stella said, looking at the dark red blood. "He may not make it to a hospital."

"He may not try," said Mac. "Flack?"

"Broken ribs. Guista sat on his chest. He should be fine," said Stella. "I called an ambulance."

"I'll go back to him," Mac said, heading back toward the apartment building. "You go back to the lab, make the calls. I . . ."

Mac's phone was ringing. He took it from his pocket and pushed the talk button. Stella hurried ahead of him toward the car parked more than a block away.

"Yes," Mac said.

"Found the bullet in the shaft," said Aiden. "You were right."

"I'll be in as soon as I can get there."

"That's not all," said Aiden. "Danny's got something you'll want to hear."

"Tell him I'm coming in," Mac said.

They met almost two hours later. It was close to seven. Aiden hadn't had her shower. Two bags of rolls and bread from Marco's Bakery in the Bronx sat untouched on the table.

After taking Flack to the hospital for X rays and to have his ribs taped, Mac had picked up gyros and drinks from a nearby Greek restaurant.

They ate slowly except for Stella, who nibbled at the crust of her pita bread.

"Heel marks in the hall at the bakery definitely came from Collier's shoes," said Danny. "I checked. He must have been strangled at the bakery."

Mac looked at Aiden.

"Bullet that killed Lutnikov was a .22," she said.

"Louisa Cormier has a .22," Mac said.

"But it hasn't been fired," Aiden responded.

"Maybe she has another one," said Mac. "Or she got rid of the one that had been fired and replaced it with the one we saw."

"Covering her ass," said Stella.

"She's a mystery writer," said Mac.

"We should have checked the registration on the gun she showed us. Do we have enough for a warrant?" asked Aiden.

"No," said Mac. "Did you notice Louisa Cormier's hands when we talked to her?"

"Clean," Aiden said with a shrug.

"Scrubbed clean," said Mac. "Her hands were red. Why?"

Mac looked around and waited.

"Lady Macbeth," said Danny.

"Mystery writer," said Stella. "Residue. Gunshot residue. She's afraid we'll find it."

Mac held up the gunshot residue information report Aiden had prepared.

During the discharge of a firearm, gases escaping

from the gun leave a residue on the shooter's hand and clothing, principally lead, barium, and antimony.

"She can't get it all off," said Aiden.

They all knew that samples would have to be taken from Louisa Cormier's skin and then examined in the lab for atomic absorption under a scanning electron microscope.

"Maybe she doesn't know she can't get it all off," said Mac. "She checks the Internet and then starts scrubbing, probably burns whatever clothing she was wearing."

"So?" asked Danny. "Can we force her to use a GSR kit on her hands?"

"Not with the evidence we have," said Aiden, "but maybe we can worry her into making a mistake."

"How?" asked Danny.

"We lie to her," said Aiden. "And Mac's the best liar I know."

"Thanks," said Mac. "First thing in the morning then. Anything new on Guista?"

"Nothing yet," said Stella.

"How's Don?" asked Danny.

"Out of the hospital," said Mac. "Doctor told him to go home, gave him pain pills. He's probably in bed by now."

Mac was wrong.

Don Flack, trying not to shiver, stood in front of the small house in Flushing, Queens and rang the bell. It was after nine. Night had dropped the temperature to just below zero degrees and that wasn't counting the wind chill.

There were lights on inside the house. He rang again, trying not to breathe deeply. The doctor who taped his ribs, Dr. Singh, had told him to take one of the hydrocodine tablets and go to bed. Don had taken half his advice. He had downed one tablet before he left the hospital.

The door opened. The warmth of the house greeted him and he found himself facing a pretty brunette teenage girl holding a book.

"Yes?" she asked.

"Is Mr. Taxx home?" he asked.

"Yes," the girl said. "I'll get him. Come in."

Flack stepped in, closing the door behind him.

"Are you all right?" the girl asked.

"I'm fine," he said.

She nodded and strode away into a room on the right calling, "Dad, there's someone here to see you."

The girl returned almost immediately to face Flack.

The warmth of the house, the stab of pain, and the hydrocodine got to the detective. He must have swayed slightly.

"Are you sick?" the girl asked.

"I'm fine," he lied.

Ed Taxx came out of the room the girl had gone into seconds earlier. He wore jeans with the cuffs rolled up and a New York Jets sweat shirt.

"Flack," he said, "you all right?"

"Fine, can we talk?"

"Sure," said Taxx. "Come on in. You want some coffee, tea, a shot of something?"

"Coffee," said Flack, following him, controlling a need to wince.

"Could you get a cup of coffee for Detective Flack?" Taxx asked the girl.

The girl nodded.

"Cream, sugar, Equal?" she asked.

"Black," said Flack as Taxx went one way and his daughter the other.

They were in a small, clean living room. The furniture wasn't new but it was bright, flowery, clean, a woman's room. Two sofas, almost matching, sat across from each other with a low gray table between them and copies of the latest *Entertainment Weekly* and *Smithsonian Magazine* next to each other.

Taxx sat on one sofa. Flack sat across from him.

"Cliff Collier's dead," Flack said.

"I got a call," Taxx said, shaking his head. "Any leads on the killer?"

"I shot the killer," said Flack straight-faced. "But he's out there someplace. He got away."

"I didn't know Collier well," said Taxx. "Just duty those two nights. You were a friend of his?"

"Went through the Academy together," said Flack, trying not to move, knowing it would result in a silent stab in his chest.

The girl came back with identical yellow mugs and cork coasters in each hand. She placed the drinks down in front of the two men.

"Thanks honey," said Taxx, smiling at his daughter.

"I'm going back to my room," she said, "unless . . ."

"Go ahead," said Taxx.

The girl looked back once and exited slowly, probably, Don thought, hoping to pick up a bit of the conversation between her father and the unexpected visitor.

"Wife's down the street playing bridge," said Taxx.

They went silent, drank their coffee.

"You in trouble?" asked Flack.

Taxx shrugged.

"DA's office is investigating," he said. "I'll probably get a reprimand and since I'll be retiring in about a year, I won't go back in the field again. Can't say it bothers me all that much. Someone has to take the blame for losing a star witness."

Flack drank. The coffee was hot but not steamy hot.

"My guess is the papers and television people will say Cliff's murder suggests that he was involved in the killing of Alberta Spanio, that he was killed to shut him up," said Don.

"I don't believe that," said Taxx, working on his own coffee. "I didn't know him well, but I was there. He didn't have anything to do with killing her."

"Then whoever did it thought Cliff saw something or knew something," said Flack. "Or figured something out. My best guess is Cliff was following a lead on his own and got spotted."

"Makes sense to me," Taxx said.

"Whoever did it may be after you next."

Taxx nodded and said, "I've been thinking about that. I can't come up with any reason."

Flack asked Taxx to go over what had happened at the hotel.

"Told you already," said Taxx. "We knocked on her door."

"We?"

"I think it was Collier who knocked. I called her name. No answer. Collier put his hand on the door and looked at me. Signaled for me to do the same. I did. The door was cold."

"Whose idea was it to break down the door?"

"We didn't discuss it," said Taxx. "We just did it. When we got in, Collier ran to the bathroom and I went to the bed to check on Alberta."

"Why did he go to the bathroom?"

"Wind was blowing in from there," said Taxx. "We just agreed, nodded, something. You know how it is when something happens fast in the field."

"Yeah," said Flack. "Why did he go to the bathroom and you to the body?"

Taxx was holding the coffee cup in his hand.

"I don't know. It just happened. I saw him run for the bathroom. That left the bed."

"How long was he in there?"

"Five, ten seconds," said Taxx. "Flack, what's going on with you? You look . . ."

"Guy who killed Cliff sat on my chest before I shot him. Broken ribs."

"You have far to drive to get here?"

"It wasn't bad."

"Want to spend the night here?" asked Taxx. "We've got an extra room."

"No, thanks," he said. "I'll be all right. When Alberta Spanio went to bed, what was the drill the last night?"

"Same as the first three nights," said Taxx. "We checked the windows to be sure they were locked."

"Who checked?"

"We both did," said Taxx.

"Who checked the bathroom window?"

"Collier. Then we left, and Alberta locked the door behind us. We heard the bolt slide and lock."

"And no sounds during the night?" asked Flack.

"From her room? No."

"From anywhere?"

"No."

"Maybe you should have someone watching your house till we pick up the guy who killed Cliff?"

"I'm well armed," said Taxx. "I know how to use my weapon."

"You might want to wear it and have it at your bedside."

Taxx pulled up his Jets sweat shirt to reveal a small holster and gun on his belt. Then he pulled the sweat shirt down.

"I got the same idea when I heard what happened to Collier, but for the life of me, I don't know what Collier and I might have heard or seen that would make Marco send out a hit on us. He's got to know the morning news will be all over this and he'll be crucified if something happens to me. More coffee?"

"No, thanks," said Flack, rising carefully.

"Sure you don't want to spend the night?"

"No, thanks," he said.

"Suit yourself," said Taxx, leading him back to the front door.

"Try to think of something you might have forgotten, missed," said Flack.

"I've been trying, going over everything, but . . . I'll keep trying," said Taxx. "Be careful out there tonight."

Flack went out the door and into the frigid night. The door closed behind him cutting off the last of the warmth. He was missing something. He knew it, felt it.

He would drive home now, carefully, knowing that the pain was winning, at least for now, at least until he got home and took another hydrocodine tablet. In the morning, he'd check in with Stella to see if she had come up with anything. Whatever else he did in the morning would depend on whether Stevie Guista had been caught.

He got into his car and reached into his jacket pocket. The move sent a shock of pain across his chest. He pulled out the bottle of pills, started to open it, and changed his mind.

It took him almost two hours to get home.

The woman on the uptown intersection video monitor was Molly Ives. She was stubby, black, studying law at night, and wide awake. Her shift, the night shift, had begun fifteen minutes earlier.

She spotted the bread truck at a red light at 96th and Third. She wasn't sure it was the one she had a note to look for on the clipboard next to her. She became sure when the light turned green and she could make out the words MARCO'S BAKERY on the side of the truck as it passed.

Molly Ives called it in to the NYPD dispatcher who contacted a patrol car in the area. Five minutes later, the patrol car cut off the bakery truck, and the two policemen inside got out.

They approached the small truck, weapons in hand, one officer on each side of the vehicle.

"Come out," called one of the officers. "Hands up."

The bakery truck door opened, and the driver climbed out slowly.

Big Stevie had stopped the bleeding. He had sat in the back of his bread truck with the heat on, took off his T-shirt and pressed it against the wound in his right leg, the thick fleshy part above the knee. When he reached back he felt the exit wound. That was bleeding less but the hole was bigger. No bones were broken. He wrapped the T-shirt tightly.

He would have to abandon the truck. He would have to see a doctor or a nurse or something. Who knows what's going on inside? Could be internal bleeding, one of those embolisms, something. And he would need money to get out of town. Steven Guista's needs were great and he had only one place to go with them.

He drove, thought about taking the bridge to Manhattan, changed his mind, and headed to the neighborhood he knew best. The makeshift bandage was holding reasonably well but some blood was seeping through. He drove to an outdoor phone, in front of a twenty-four-hour grocery where he had stopped a few dozen times before. He parked and hobbled out of the truck.

"It's me," he said when the woman answered. He gave her the number of the phone he was calling from. She hung up. He stood, shivering, light-headed, waiting, the lights of the grocery giving off no heat. She called back in ten minutes.

"Where are you?" she asked.

"Brooklyn," he said. "Went back to my place. Cop shot me."

The pause was so long that Stevie asked, "You there?"

"I'm here," she said. "How badly hurt are you?"

"Leg," he said. "I need a doctor."

"I'll give you an address," she said. "Can you remember it?"

"I don't have a pencil, paper, anything," he said.

"Then just keep saying it to yourself. Get rid of the truck. Take a cab."

She gave him the name of a woman, Lynn Contranos, and an address. He repeated them to her.

"I'll call her and tell her you're coming."

The woman hung up. Stevie pulled change out of his pocket, dialed information for a car service number, made the call, and waited. While he waited he almost sang the name of the woman he was supposed to see, Lynn Contranos.

His birthday was only a few hours from ending. He didn't want to think about it. His pants were sticking to his leg now, the blood freezing.

He kept repeating the mantra as he waited, didn't think beyond going to that address. One thing at a time and maybe he would come out of this.

There was no car fifteen minutes later, and Big Stevie got back in the bread truck, turned on the heat and waited, watching the curb for the arrival of the car.

If it doesn't get here in ten more minutes, I'm driving. He was having trouble remembering the name and address he was supposed to go to, but he kept repeating them as he waited for the car that might never come.

Mac sat in his living room in the worn brown chair with the matching ottoman. His wife had indulged him. He had loved the chair, was still drawn to it, but the love was gone. It was just a place to sit and work or watch a ball game or a dog show or an old movie.

Tonight, clad in a clean gray sweat suit, it was work. On the slightly scratched, inlaid wooden table by his side stood two piles of books, new, fresh smelling, and twenty-seven neatly typed pages of paper clipped together. On a small cutting board no larger than one of the books rested a mug of coffee he had just microwaved.

There was also a stack of book reviews, old and new, he had printed from the Internet.

It was just before ten.

He had the books by Louisa Cormier arranged in chronological order. Her first book was titled *Genesis Standing*. The reviews had been mildly good, but the sales had been phenomenal. By the fourth book, reviews said Louisa Cormier had turned a corner and belonged among the upper echelon of mystery writers. Now she was always compared, favorably, with women writers like Sue Grafton, Mary Higgins Clark, Marcia Muller, Faye Kellerman, and Sara Paretsky.

Mac took a sip of coffee. It wasn't hot enough, but he didn't want to get up, go to the kitchen and go through the microwaving process again. He drank a little deeper and hoped he found the work of Louisa Cormier interesting.

Before he could open the first book, the phone rang.

It was a little after ten at night. Stella was looking over Danny's shoulder as he constructed the image on the computer screen in the lab.

Stella's eyes burned. She no longer doubted that she was coming down with something. Something was definitely causing her sinuses to fill, her eyes to water, and her throat to tickle. She tried to ignore it.

The image on the screen looked like something out of one of those computer generated games advertised on television, the ones in which people, who didn't look all that much like people, slaughtered each other with noisy weapons, vicious kicks, and painful sounds.

On the screen was a computer-generated brick wall. There was a single window in the wall.

"How high above the bathroom window was the window to Guista's hotel room?" he asked.

"Twelve feet," Stella answered.

Danny's fingers played the keys and moved the mouse until the image scrolled down. A second window suddenly appeared.

"Reduce it so we can see both windows," Stella said.

Danny did it. One window was now directly above the other.

"It was night," she reminded him.

Danny created night.

"Was the bathroom light on?" he asked.

Stella pulled out her notes and a small packet of tissues. She flipped through the notes and said, "She slept with the bathroom light on."

"Bathroom light on," Danny said.

And a light yellow glow appeared in the lower window.

"Now the chain from Guista's room to the bathroom," Stella said wiping her nose.

"Chains, chains, chains, chains," Danny said pushing his glasses back on his nose and searching. "Here. Pick a chain."

He scrolled down.

"This one's close to the one he used," Danny said.

"Can you make it hang from Guista's window down to the bathroom?" Stella asked.

"You are definitely coming down with something," he said.

"If he used the chain to lower someone," she said, instead of responding to his comment, "the person would have to be small, brave, and hope that the bathroom window was open."

"Or know that it was open," Danny said.

"Can you put a person at the end of the chain?"

A figure, male, dressed like a ninja, appeared.

"Make him smaller," she said.

Danny made the figure smaller.

"Can you open the window?" she asked.

"How wide was it open?"

She consulted her notes again and came up with, "A little under fourteen inches."

Danny opened the window to scale.

"Narrow," he said. "Should I make our ninja smaller?"

"Sure," she said.

Done.

"By scale, how much would you say he or she weighs now?" asked Stella.

Danny sat back, thought, and said, "Maybe one hundred," he said. "Maximum one hundred and ten."

"And he had to open the window and swing through it," Stella said.

"And he had to get back out through the window with that clearance," said Danny. "An acrobat? Maybe we should be checking on gymnasts and circus acrobats?"

Stella thought and said, "Can you put something into the lower part of the window, where we found the screw hole?"

"Something?"

"A circular piece of metal?"

"How big a circle?"

"Start big, five inch diameter."

Danny searched. An image appeared at the bottom of the bathroom window. A circle.

"Can you make it stand out, perpendicular to the window?" she asked.

"I can try."

He manipulated the circle, give it a three-dimensional hoop look.

They both looked at the chain, the hoop, and the window and came to the same conclusion.

"You going to say it or should I?" he asked.

"Get rid of the ninja," she said.

"Check," said Danny, and the ninja was gone.

"Attach the end of the chain to the hoop," she said.

He was ahead of her and had it done before she had finished his sentence.

"Guista hooked the hoop and then kept pulling till the hoop on the screw came out," said Danny, showing it on screen as they watched. "That's what happened. It also explains why he used a metal chain instead of a rope. A rope would flop in the wind. A chain with a hook would be easier to grab the hoop. And then he lowered whoever killed Alberta Spanio."

"Why couldn't the killer just open the window and climb in?" Stella asked, looking at the computer screen. "Why go through this hoop and chain business? Maybe the killer didn't come through the window."

"Why would someone go through all that to open a window they weren't going to use?" asked Danny.

"Maybe to bring the temperature down below freezing in the bedroom so we couldn't pinpoint time of death?"

"Why do that?"

Stella shrugged.

"Maybe they wanted to make it look as if someone had come through the window," Danny said. "But the snow screwed that up."

"We're still missing something," Stella said, followed by a sneeze.

"Cold," he said. "Maybe flu."

"Allergies," Stella answered. "We've got to find Guista and get some answers out of him."

"If he's still alive," said Danny.

"If he's still alive," Stella repeated.

"I've got some Vitamin C tablets in my kit," Danny said. "Want one?"

"Make it three," she said.

Danny stood, still looking at the image on the screen.

"What?" Stella asked.

"Maybe we're wrong," he said. "Maybe somebody did go down that chain."

"The little man the clerk saw with Guista," she said.

"Back to square one?" said Danny.

"Database?"

"Looking for the little man," said Danny. "Let's go home and start again in the morning."

Normally, Stella would have said something like, "Go ahead, I have a few things to clean up." But not tonight. She was one large ache, and home sounded good to her.

They both went home. When they came in the next morning, they would have information that threatened to throw their theory out of the window.

The two black kids who stepped out of the bakery truck, hands in the air, couldn't have been more than fifteen.

The police officers, one a black woman named Clea Barnes, kept their weapons leveled at the driver. Her partner, Barney Royce, was ten years older than Clea and not nearly as good a shot. He was and always had been just average on the range. Fortunately, in his twenty-six years in uniform, he had never had to shoot at anyone. Clea, however, with four years in, had already shot three perps. None had died. Barney figured punks and drunks took Clea for an easy mark. They were wrong.

"Step away from the truck," Barney ordered.

"We didn't do nothin'," the driver said in a surly manner both police officers well recognized.

"No," said Clea. "You didn't do nothing. You did something. Where'd you get this truck?"

The two boys, both wearing black winter coats and no caps or hats, looked at the truck as if they had not noticed it before.

"This truck?" said the driver as Barney moved forward to check both of the boys for weapons. They were clean.

"That truck," Clea said patiently.

"Friend let us drive it," the driver said.

"Tell us about your friend," said Barney.

"A friend," said the driver with a shrug.

"Name, color," said Clea.

"White dude," said the driver. "Didn't catch his name."

"You didn't know his name but he let you take the truck," said Barney.

"That's right," said the boy.

"One chance," said Clea. "We bring you in, get your prints, check you out, let you walk if you tell us the truth. Right now. No bullshit."

The boy shook his head and looked at his buddy.

The second boy spoke for the first time.

"We were in Brooklyn," he said. "Visiting some friends. On the way to the subway, we saw this big old white guy walking around. Limping around in front of a deli. It wasn't a neighborhood where you'd expect to find a white guy walking around, big guy or not."

"So you decided to rob him?" Barney asked.

"I didn't say that. Besides, while we were talking, a cab pulled up. He got in. We checked out the truck when the cab was gone. Keys were in the truck."

"And you took it?" asked Clea.

"Beats the subway," the first kid said.

"Where was this deli in Brooklyn?" asked Barney.

"Flatbush Avenue," the second kid told them. "J.V.'s Deli."

"Now," said Clea. "Big question that's going to maybe let you walk if you're not wanted for something: What kind of cab was it and what time did the white guy get picked up."

The second boy smiled and said, "One of those car

service sedans. Green Cab Number 4304. Picked him up a few minutes after nine."

Aiden had taken her shower, washed her hair, put on her warmest pajamas, and turned on the television in her bedroom. *The Daily Show* would be on in half an hour. Meanwhile she turned on CNN and lay back with a pad of paper, glancing up from time to time at the news scroll at the bottom of the screen.

On the pad she wrote:

One, call Cormier's agent. Ask about .22 she supposedly gave her. Ask about the manuscripts she delivers. On disk? Printed out?

Two, is there enough for a search warrant of Cormier's apartment? Check it out with Mac.

Three, more research on Cormier's background.

Four, check with all the tenants who use the elevator. See if they own .22s. Could be wrong about Cormier. Don't think so.

There hadn't been much left of the bullet, but there was enough to match with a weapon if one could be found.

She half listened to *The Daily Show*, trying to think if there was something she had missed. She made a few more notes when the show was over, switched to ABC to see what was on *Nightline*. It was about whether serial killers were evil. Guests were going to be a lawyer, an FBI profiler, a psychologist, and a psychiatrist.

Aiden switched off the television with her remote. She knew that evil existed. She had witnessed it, sat across the table from it. There was a difference between someone being crazy and someone being evil.

Evil was not an acceptable diagnosis for a killer. There was no clinical description for it, no number assigned it. There were dozens of variations, all psychological, in the reference books for serial killers, brutal one- or two-time murderers, child molesters, but none of them could cope with the reality of someone being simply, clearly evil.

She didn't want to go down that road before she got some sleep, didn't want to go down through the death penalty arguments again. If someone was, indeed, evil, there was no cure, no treatment. You either lock them up forever when you catch them or you execute them.

She turned off the lights and was asleep almost instantly.

Big Stevie didn't give the driver the exact address where he was going. He didn't want him to write it down, remember it. He gave him an address a block away instead. He would have made it two blocks, but he didn't trust his throbbing leg.

It was a risk. Stevie had been repeating the address to himself and was afraid of losing it if he gave the driver a different address, but Stevie had to be careful. Mr. Marco would want him to be careful.

When the car stopped, Stevie paid the driver and gave him a decent tip, not too big, not too small. Stevie made a painful effort not to limp or wince, not to be remembered.

The driver took off as soon as Stevie closed the door. He didn't ask if he should wait. Stevie found himself in a vaguely familiar area of Brooklyn Heights. There was no one on the sidewalk, no cars passing by on the narrow street. There were tightly packed together three-story brownstones and granite buildings. Garbage was stacked next to mounds of snow. Both sides of the street looked fortified with makeshift walls of snow and garbage.

Stevie was on the opposite side of the street from his destination. He limped along, growing weaker with each step, knowing the bleeding had started again, that he had probably left blood on the seat of the car. Couldn't be helped.

He was about to cross the street when he noticed another car. It was parked ahead of him on his side of the street. The windows were steamy. The motor was idling quietly.

He thought he could make out two figures in the front seat but he wasn't sure because of the steamy windows. Were they watching the entrance to the brownstone where he was headed?

Cops? No, couldn't be. Maybe they weren't looking for him. Maybe they were just waiting for someone else or stopping to talk about something or . . . Stevie didn't buy it. What had happened to him today made him think. He preferred to have others think for him, others he could trust, like Marco, but that was the problem. He was beginning to distrust Marco.

Think it through, he said to himself as he stepped into the shadows of a dark doorway where he could keep his eyes on the two people in the car.

I did the job at the hotel. I killed a cop. I busted up another cop. If I get picked up, Marco might worry about my talking. He should know better, but he might worry. Could I blame him? Yes.

He couldn't wait. Stevie had to get somewhere where he could be patched up. He was bleeding again, and not a little bit.

Take a chance with Lynn Contranos? He didn't know her. Think of someplace else to go? He had no real options. Well, maybe one, but he would avoid it if he could. He crossed the street and headed for the brownstone. He didn't look back, but he heard the car door open and close behind him.

He found the name on a plastic plate on the stone wall, LYNN CONTRANOS, MASSAGE THERAPIST. He pressed the button, sensing the two people approaching him. No answer. He pressed the button again and a woman's voice came through the small speaker, "Yes?"

"Steven Guista," he said.

"Be right there," she said, her voice muffled, and clicked off.

Did he recognize that voice? Stevie wasn't sure. A few seconds later he heard a metal ping coming from the front door. He reached for the door handle sensing now that the two people were only a few feet behind him. Instead of opening the door, Big Stevie turned quickly, surprising them, two men, both of them much younger than Stevie, neither of them as large. One of the men had a gun in his right hand.

Stevie recognized both of them. One was a baker's assistant at Marco's. The other was the bakery security guard. It was the security guard who held the gun.

Stevie didn't hesitate. His fist pounded deeply into the stomach of the man with the gun who doubled forward. At the same time, with his free hand Stevie reached out for the neck of the second man who was groping for something in his pocket.

Stevie forgot about the pain in his leg and concentrated on simply staying alive.

11

"WHO?" asked Danny the next morning after Stella finished reading the E-mail message on the screen in front of her.

Danny hadn't slept well. He dreamt of a chain dangling in the cold wind and himself slowly sliding down it, trying to hold on, his hands slipping, knowing he would eventually run out of chain and fall into the darkness below him. It was a long dream. He remembered calling out for help below but no one could hear him at that distance in the darkness and the whistling wind. He had been happy to get out of bed at five and get to work.

"Jacob Laudano," Stella said.

Danny looked over her shoulder at the screen and read out loud, "Jacob the Jockey?"

"That's what he's called," she said.

"He's a jockey?"

"Was," she said.

"Which means . . ." Danny began.

"He's probably small," said Stella. "Let's . . ."

She used the mouse and hit more keys.

"The last time he was pulled in, that was last August, he stood four ten and weighed ninety pounds. Look at his rap sheet."

Danny looked. The list was long and included an arrest for stabbing a prostitute and five other arrests for bar fights, all involving knives.

"Laudano is a known associate of Steven Guista," said Stella.

"What do we do?" he asked.

"Attach a ninety-pound weight to that chain," she said. "Lower it twelve feet and see if it holds."

"We'll need more chain," said Danny.

"We'll need more chain," Stella agreed. "But that can wait. Guista's bakery truck was picked up last night. It's at an impound on Staten Island."

"So we're going there first?" asked Danny.

Stella shook her head "no" and said, "First we go to Brooklyn."

"Brooklyn," Danny repeated. "Why?"

"Guista took a car service from a location in Brooklyn last night," said Stella, reaching for a report next to her desk and handing it to Danny. "We check the company. Find out where he went. Should be easy. One of the two kids who took Guista's truck for a spin remembered Guista, the time and the car."

"It's going to be a busy day," said Danny. "What about Laudano, the Jockey?"

"Flack is on it," she said.

"He should be in bed," said Danny.

"He should be in the hospital," said Stella, "but he's not. He's on the street. Let's go."

"Since we're on the subject of hospitals," he said. "You're not looking any better."

"I'm fine."

"Your face is red," he said. "You have a fever."

She ignored his comment and put the computer in sleep mode, dropped a small stack of reports in a file folder, and stood up.

"The Jockey," Danny said almost to himself. "Who would have thought? It makes no sense."

"Why not?" asked Stella, leading the way out of the lab.

"A crooked union boss with mob connections hires a circus act to murder a witness? A strong man and a . . ." Don asked.

"Little person," Stella completed.

"Why?" asked Danny. "They were sure to be noticed."

Stella picked up her kit in one hand and her file folder in the other. Danny took her place at the computer.

"Maybe we're supposed to think it's a circus act," she said.

"Red herring?" asked Danny.

"It smells fishy," she said with a smile.

Danny groaned.

Stella left the lab, went to the elevator, and pushed the button for the lobby. Stella coughed, a raspy cough.

"Why?" said Louisa Cormier's agent, Michelle King, a twitchy woman in her late forties. Like Louisa she was well groomed, thin, and dressed for business in a black suit and white blouse. She did not have her client's good looks, but she made up for it with a handsome, confident severity. The room smelled of cigarettes and a flowered spray scent.

Aiden sat in one chair of King's office on Madison Avenue. King played with a pencil, tapping it impatiently against the top of her mahogany desk.

"Why?" Michelle King asked again.

Mac looked at her for ten seconds and said, "We can go to our offices and discuss this. I don't think you'd like it there. Dead bodies and evidence from things people don't like to touch or even see."

"I did advise Louisa to get a gun and keep it loaded in her apartment," Michelle King said, reaching for a cigarette in a packet in one of her desk drawers.

"You mind?" she asked, unsteadily holding up the cigarette.

"We won't arrest you for it, if that's what you're asking," Mac said. Smoking was illegal in New York City buildings. "Besides, many of the people we have to deal with smoke," Mac said. "We accept it. One of the hazards of the job."

"Second-hand smoke?" Michelle King asked lighting up with a silver-plated lighter. "It's a myth created by anti-smoking fanatics who have nothing better to do."

"And first-hand murder," said Mac. "Is that a myth?"

The agent looked at Aiden, who said nothing, which seemed to unnerve King more than Mac's questions.

"All right," King said. "I advised her to get a gun, even suggested the kind she might get, one just like mine."

"Can we look at yours?" asked Mac.

"You think I shot that man?" she asked, blowing out a plume of smoke and pausing in her pencil tapping.

"We know he's dead," said Mac.

"Why on earth would Louisa or I want to kill this man, whoever he was?"

"His name was Charles Lutnikov," said Aiden. "He was a writer."

"Never heard of him," King said, putting out her cigarette.

"Your name and phone number were in his address book," said Mac.

"My—?" King said.

"He called your office three times last week," said Aiden. "It's in his phone records."

"I never spoke to him," King insisted.

"Your secretary?" asked Mac.

"Wait, the name does ring a bell," said King. "I think that may have been the name of the person who kept leaving his number. The message from Amy, my assistant, was that he said he had something important to tell me."

"But you didn't call him back?"

She shrugged.

"Amy said he sounded nervous, was very insistent and . . . well, I'm an agent. I've got lots of oddballs wanting to talk to me about their ideas for books. One of Amy's jobs is to keep them away from me."

"But this oddball lived in the same apartment building as one of your biggest clients," said Aiden.

"My biggest client," King corrected. "I was unaware of that."

She reached into her desk drawer suddenly and came up with a small gun which she pointed at Aiden. Neither detective flinched.

"My gun," King said, handing it across her desk.

Mac took it and handed it to Aiden who examined it and said, "Never been fired."

"Not even loaded," said King. "It's like a chenille blanket I had when I was a little girl. I keep it around for comfort and a sense of security, which I delude myself is real."

"What happens to the manuscripts of Louisa Cormier's books after she gives them to you?" Mac asked.

"She doesn't give me manuscripts," said King. "She E-mails me her manuscripts as attachments. I read them and send them on to her editor. Louisa's work requires very little editing by me or the publisher."

King picked up the pencil again, considered tapping it, changed her mind, and put it down.

"What about the first three books," said Mac.

King looked at him warily.

"The first three books were . . . a little rough," King said. "They needed work. How did you know?"

"I read them last night, as well as the fourth and fifth," said Mac. "Something changed."

"With experience and confidence, Louisa's work, I'm pleased to say, has steadily improved," said King.

"Do you keep her books on your hard drive?" asked Mac.

"I have hard copies made in addition to disk copies of all Louisa's books," King said.

"We'd like to borrow the disks," Mac said.

"I'll have Amy make copies for you," she said, "but why would you—"

"We won't take any more of your time right now," said Mac, rising.

Aiden got up too.

King remained seated.

"We'll be in touch," said Mac, going to the door.

"I sincerely hope not," said King, reaching for her cigarettes.

When they got past the reception area and into the hall, Aiden said, "She's lying."

"About?"

"Those first books," said Aiden.

Mac nodded.

"You noticed," she said.

"She's protecting her golden calf," said Mac.

"So?" asked Aiden.

"Let's go see Louisa Cormier."

Stella saw the red, amoeba-shaped splotch of blood on a low snowbank on the sidewalk next to a black plastic garbage bag.

The driver, a Nigerian named George Apappa, had taken her to the spot where he had dropped the man who had bled on his backseat. George had noticed the blood as soon as he got to his home in Jackson Heights. He couldn't miss the blood. The man had left a small puddle on the floor and a dark, still-moist streak on the seat.

It had taken George almost an hour to clean the bloodstains. He got into bed with his wife at two in the morning and the phone rang at six—his dispatcher, telling him to get into the garage immediately. He told Stella all this with the sound of a man who had planned to sleep until noon, but instead had dragged himself out of bed, half expecting to be told he was fired when he got to the garage. Stella had a feeling the twenty she slipped him would help him get over his lack of sleep.

Stella could feel him watching her from the car as she wiped her nose and took a picture of the mound of snow, then scooped up some of the snow with a shovel and dropped it in a plastic bag.

She started to move slowly along the sidewalk, pausing every few steps to take another photograph. The trail of blood was reasonably easy to follow, frozen in place. Few pedestrians had yet trampled the icy sidewalk.

Stella put the back of her left hand against her forehead and felt both moisture and fever. She had a thermometer in her kit, but it was reserved for the dead. She had taken three aspirin back at the lab along with a glass of orange juice. She had no hope for this remedy.

It took her four minutes to find the doorway. There were blood splatters on the door, not thick, but visible. There was blood on the doorstop and something yellowish-brown that looked like vomit. She took photographs, got a sample of the yellow-brown goop, and started to stand when she noticed a spot of white in the crevice of the concrete step. She knelt again. It was a tooth, a bloody tooth. She bagged it and rose to check the listing of the names of the tenants of the building lined up, white on black, near the right side of the door. The names meant nothing to her. She wrote all six down in her notebook.

Whatever had happened here had happened just before ten, according to the driver's log. It was possible someone inside had heard whatever it was that caused someone to vomit and lose what looked like a reasonably healthy tooth.

Stella rubbed her hands together and called Danny Messer at the lab.

"Check out these names," she said. "Got a pen?"

"You sound terrible," he said.

"I sound terrible," she agreed. "The names."

She read off the names slowly, spelling each one.

"Got it," he said.

"Check them all out. If you find something, call me back. Guista may have been on his way to see one of them last night when something went wrong."

"What?" he asked.

"I'm sending what I've got over to you with a cabbie," she said. "Pay my fare. I've already given him a tip."

Stella tried to hold back a cough. She couldn't do it.

"Stella . . ." Danny started, but she cut him off.

"Got to go."

She clicked off and went to the car where George

Apappa sat, head back, eyes closed. She opened her kit, dropped the digital disk of photos, the blood samples, the bloody tooth, and the clump of vomit, all separately bagged, into a zippered insulated bag. Then she opened the driver's side door.

George awoke and had the bag in his hand before he could speak.

She gave him the CSI address and told him to put the bag directly in the hands of Daniel Messer, who would be waiting for it. Messer, she said, would pay whatever the charge was. She handed him a ten dollar bill on top of that.

There was a beat in which she saw George wanted to ask what this was all about, but he didn't. He placed the bag on the seat next to him as Stella closed the door.

This time when Louisa Cormier opened the door for Mac and Aiden she was not quite so bright and bubbling. She looked as if she hadn't slept and she was wearing what looked like an oversized flowered smock. Her hair was in place, as was her make-up, but not as perfect as the day before.

She stepped back to let them in.

"Michelle, my agent, called to tell me I should expect you," she said.

Neither Mac nor Aiden spoke.

"You suspect me of having killed that man in the elevator," she said calmly.

Mac and Aiden were expressionless.

"Please, let's sit," said Louisa. "Coffee? Good manners die hard. Unfortunate choice of words, but . . ."

"No, thank you," Mac said for both of them.

The three stood just inside the door.

"Well I was just having one so if you don't mind . . ." she said and headed for the kitchen. "Please, have a seat."

Mac and Aiden moved to the table by the window. A cold fog had settled over Manhattan. There wasn't much to see besides a few lights through the dense gray and the peaks of skyscrapers over the cloud.

"I'm sorry," Louisa Cormier said, cup of steaming coffee in hand, sitting at the table in the same seat she had been in the day before. "I've been up all night working. Michelle may have told you I have a book due by the end of the week, not that my publisher will do anything about my being late, but I'm never late. Writing for a living is a job. I think it's wrong to be late for work. Sorry, I'm rambling a bit. I'm tired and I've just been told I'm a murder suspect."

"Gun residue," said Mac.

"I know what it is," she said. "Bits, traces of powder left when a gun has been fired."

"It's hard to clean off," said Aiden.

Both CSI investigators looked at Louisa Cormier's hands. They were scrubbed red.

"You want to check my hands for gunpowder residue?" she asked.

"Gunpowder residue can be transferred from a person's hand to another object they touch," said Mac.

"Interesting," said Louisa, working on her coffee.

"When we were here yesterday, you touched a few things," Mac continued.

Louisa was alert now.

"You stole something from my apartment?" she said.

Mac ignored the question. He was giving her as little as possible. Neither he nor Aiden had taken anything.

"You fired a gun recently," Aiden said.

Mac thought he detected the hint of a smile on the author's face.

"You have no way of knowing that," said Louisa. "You've not examined my hands and I doubt you would take an item of my clothing without a warrant."

Aiden and Mac did not respond.

"However," Louisa said, "you may do so. I think you will find residue on my right hand. I fired a gun at a nearby range two days ago, just before the storm. I think I should call my lawyer," Louisa said with a smile.

"Press will find out," said Mac. "But you have the right to call a lawyer before you answer any more questions."

Louisa Cormier hesitated.

"I told you I did fire a weapon," she said. "I test all the weapons I use in my books. Weight, noise, kickback, size. I was at the range two days ago. I told you. It's Drietch's on Fifty-eighth Street. I'll give you the address. You can check with Mathew Drietch."

"What was the weapon?" Aiden asked.

"A .22," she said.

"Like the one in your desk," said Mac.

"Exactly. I decided to write about a weapon like the one I own," she said.

"Lutnikov was killed with a .22," said Mac.

"I found the bullet at the bottom of the elevator shaft," said Aiden.

"We'll find a weapon," said Mac. "And we'll match the bullet to it. You said you didn't own any gun but the one you showed us yesterday," said Mac.

"I don't," Louisa answered. "Mathew Drietch has a gun just like mine. He has hundreds of guns. You can chose the one you want to use. Mr. Drietch was quite happy to let me do so."

"You wouldn't know where that .22 is now, would you?" asked Mac.

"I presume it's safely locked away at the firing range," said Louisa.

"You mind if we search your apartment?" asked Mac. "We can get a warrant."

"I do mind if you search my apartment," she said, "but if you get your warrant and do so, you'll find no weapon here other than the gun in my desk, which you know has not been fired recently."

"One more question," said Mac.

"No more questions," Louisa said gently. "My lawyer's name is Lindsey Terry. He's in the phone book. I'm sorry if I'm a bit edgy but I haven't slept and . . ."

"I read some of your books last night," Mac said.

"Oh," said Louisa. "Which ones?"

"Another Woman's Nightmare, Woman in the Dark, A Woman's Place," said Mac.

"My first three," Louisa said. "Did you like them?"

"They got better after those three," he said.

"I've always thought the first three were my best," said Louisa. "Did You read the others?"

"Two of them," said Mac.

"You're a fast reader."

"I did a lot of skimming. I'm asking a professor of linguistics at Columbia to take a look at your books," Mac said.

"What on earth for?" Louisa said.

"I think you know," said Mac.

"You have my lawyer's name," Louisa said somberly. "Now if you'll excuse me, I've got to finish my book and get some rest."

When Aiden and Mac were in the small reception area in front of the elevator, Aiden said, "She did it."

"She did it," Mac agreed. "Now let's prove it."

They started toward the front entrance, footsteps a chill echo. In front of them, about twenty yards away, stood a lean man in his late twenties or early thirties. The expressionless, pale, clean-shaven man in jeans and a blue T-shirt and a down Eddie Bauer jacket had his hands folded in front of him as he watched Aiden and Mac approach.

When the detectives were a few yards away from him, he stepped in their path.

"You're investigating the murder of Charles Lutnikov," he said, his voice even, speaking slowly.

"That's right," said Mac.

"I killed him," the man said.

He was trembling.

*   *   *

"How are you doing?" Stella asked, standing back a few feet so she wouldn't breathe on Danny.

She was sick, no doubt about it. Temperature, chills, slight nausea.

Nausea was no stranger to CSI investigators, and Stella was no exception. She seldom wore a mask at a crime scene no matter how foul the smell, no matter how long a body had lain in a bathtub bloating and emitting up a putrid, familiar stench.

The last time she had held back the unplanned rush of bile had been two weeks earlier when she and Aiden had gone to the home of a cat lady in a brownstone on the East Side. A uniformed cop had been at the door, a look of disgust on his face, which he made no attempt to hide.

Stella and Aiden had gone in and been hit by the reek, the sound of dozens of cats howling, and a sweltering heat from radiators along the walls. The dark room smelled of death, urine and feces.

"Let's not play macho," Stella had said.

Aiden had nodded and they had put on the masks in their kit and made their way to the bedroom where they found the corpse of the old woman in the print dress. Dried vomit was on her chest. Wide eyes stared at the ceiling. Something crawled at the edge of her mouth, and a large orange cat sat on her distended stomach and hissed at the two women.

"Check with the officer," said Stella. "If he hasn't called Animal Control, have him do it now."

With that and the sound of her own voice speaking inside her, Stella reminded herself that this was what she did, what had to be done, and that she did it better than anyone else.

And so she had spent an hour in the filth, which had begun to accumulate long before the woman died. An examination of the body by Hawkes showed that the woman, who looked as if she had been strangled, had instead died after a heart attack, which caused her to choke on her own vomit.

Danny's back was turned to her. He held up a corked test tube with a yellow viscous liquid inside.

"Last time," he said. "You're sick. You should be in bed."

"It's a cold," she said.

He shook his head.

"I'm taking care of it. I had some tea," she said.

"One small step for mankind," he said.

Stella ignored him and asked, "What did you find?"

"Whoever produced this vomit, should change his diet," said Danny. "He's using his stomach to store and process fat. He had both pepperoni and some kind of sausage, also a large quantity of pasta with a spicy sauce that on a scale of one to ten I'd give an *ah caramba*."

"Danny," Stella said with barely veiled impatience.

"Flour," Danny said. "Unprocessed, unbleached. This guy has been breathing in flour."

"You tested the flour?" she said, holding back a sniffle.

"Traces in the vomit. Marco's Bakery. Perfect match to our sample," he said.

"And the rubber marks in the hallway of the bakery definitely match the heels of Collier's shoes?" asked Stella.

"All trails lead back to Marco's Bakery," he said.

He put the test tube down and turned to her.

"Mind if I make a clinical observation?" he said. He didn't wait for an answer. "Your nose is as red as a maraschino cherry."

"Stella the red-nosed CSI investigator," she said.

"No kidding," Danny said. "You should be—"

"I thought you said you were finished with playing doctor," she said.

Danny shrugged.

"Want to know about the blood work?" she asked.

He nodded.

"As expected, most of the samples from the sidewalk and the doorway match Guista's," she said. "He's losing a lot of blood. If he hasn't already, he'll pass out soon if he doesn't get to a doctor. But there's also blood from someone else."

Danny sat on a lab stool. Stella sank slowly into another one.

"Guista gets shot by Flack," she said. "He drives his bakery truck to Brooklyn, abandons the truck in front of a deli, takes a car. Gets out and walks half a block. Someone's waiting for him."

"And someone gets a surprise," said Danny. "My guess: Guista hits him hard. He throws up, bleeds, loses a tooth. Guista's on the run again. Or on a slow walk."

Stella nodded and said, "Something like that. The kids who took the bakery truck said he used the telephone. Did you check the call?"

Danny shook his head. "I'll check it now. You go home."

The look she gave him made Danny decide to end his crusade to get Stella to take care of herself. Finally.

"Did you check the names of the people in that apartment building?"

"Thought you'd never ask," said Danny. "All but one has an arrest record."

"So—" Stella began.

"The one without the arrest record is a Lynn Contranos," he said.

"You look absolutely glutinous with self approbation," Stella said.

"With . . . ?"

"It's from a Hitchcock movie," she said, wiping her nose. "What about her?"

"Lynn Contranos aka Helen Grandfield," he said. "Dario Marco's trusted assistant."

Stella nodded.

"But that's not all," Danny said adjusting his glasses, eager. "Helen Grandfield's name, before she married Stanley Contranos, who is doing a minimum of ten to twenty for Murder Two, was Helen Marco, niece of Anthony Marco who is on trial as we speak. Ergo, Dario Marco is her father."

"All roads lead back to Marco's Bakery," said Stella. "Let's pay them another visit."

"And take a couple of uniforms with us?" he asked.

Stella nodded and reached into her pocket for the small plastic bottle of tablets Sheldon Hawkes had given her less than an hour ago.

"Might make you more tired," Hawkes had said. "But it'll numb you down."

She opened the bottle.

The name of the young man who had confessed to the murder of Charles Lutnikov was Jordan Breeze, who lived on the third floor of the Belvedere Towers in a studio apartment. Breeze, a Drexel University graduate, was a computer programmer for an Indian company on 55th Street. His job was to create software programs to help track and map the universe.

Mac looked up from the folder in his hands into the eyes of Jordan Breeze and then back at the folder. Breeze had never been in trouble with the police, didn't belong to any radical groups. After questioning the neighbors, Mac had determined that he was a quiet tenant who always had a "good morning" for others. However, he had been seen less and less over the past few months. A number of other tenants had seen him at the Starbucks two blocks away working on his computer and a Grande Latte, but not for a while. Mac turned on the tape recorder.

"You're sure you don't want a lawyer?" Mac asked.

"Certain," said Breeze.

"Why did you kill him?" asked Mac.

"He called me a queer," said Breeze. "Not just once. Many times. I shuddered when I left my apartment in the morning or went back in the evening, afraid I'd run into him. I see the question in your eyes."

"What question?" asked Mac.

"Am I gay," said Breeze. "I'm not, but some of my friends are, and I'm not going to suffer homophobic fools. I took it for almost a year."

"And then," said Mac. "You killed him. How?"

"With a gun," said Breeze. "He was on the elevator. I could have avoided him if I had chosen to go down the stairs, but he would have seen me."

"You had the gun with you?" asked Mac.

"I did."

"You planned to kill him the next time he started in on you?"

"Yes," said Breeze. "I got in the elevator. The doors closed. He started . . ."

"He called me a skinny-ass fag," said Breeze. "The gun was in the outer pocket of my computer case. There is some shit I will not eat."

Mac nodded, looked at the file folder again and then up at Jordan Breeze.

"Where did you get the gun?" he asked.

"It was my father's," said Breeze. "He died a few years ago, cancer."

"What kind of gun?"

"A .22 millimeter."

"What were you doing on the elevator to the upper floors?"

"I followed Lutnikov when he got off and changed elevators," said Breeze. "He seemed surprised and amused."

"You got on the elevator because you planned to kill him," said Mac.

"Yes."

"What did you do with the gun after you killed Charles Lutnikov?"

"Got off the elevator and sent it up. Then I trudged happily through the snow to the East River and threw it in," said Breeze. "It went through a thin layer of ice. I threw the leather gloves I was wearing into the river too. I'm afraid you have me on charges of murder and polluting the river."

"How many times did you shoot Lutnikov?"

"Twice," said Breeze. "Once when he was standing and again when he fell."

"The doorman doesn't remember you going out," Mac said.

"I waited till the afternoon and lots of people were going in and out."

"How well do you know Louisa Cormier?" asked Mac.

"Never met her," he said. "Don't even know if I've even seen her in the building. I know she's in the penthouse. I haven't been in the building that long."

"Do you mind if we look at your apartment? We can get a warrant."

"Please," said Breeze, "by all means examine my apartment and check my storage locker in the basement."

There was a calm smile on Breeze's face, close to the contented smile of cult members who are certain they know the truth about life and have reduced its mystery to a simple loyalty.

Mac turned off the tape recorder, rose, and went to the door. As he opened it, Breeze stood on shaking legs.

When Jordan Breeze had been taken away, Aiden entered the interrogation room where Mac sat tapping the thin folder on the table.

"You don't think he did it?" she said.

"I'll look into it. If he didn't do it, someone gave him a lot of information on the killing," said Mac. "And we keep on the with the investigation of Louisa Cormier."

"You could be wrong," she said.

"I could be," Mac agreed.

12

STEVIE COULDN'T GET THE FIRST CAR he tried to start. It had been almost fifty years since he had boosted a car. Sometimes you do forget how to ride a bicycle.

The car was a green Ford Escort parked half a block from where he had left the two men from the bakery, one doubled over in pain, the other trying to stop the bleeding from his nose. He had been sure they were hurt too badly to try to follow him. He had considered killing them both, but that would leave two bodies. Better to let them crawl away.

The problem was that Stevie also had to almost crawl away. He was losing blood and trying to think of where he could go.

One of the back doors of the Escort had been open, the lock broken. Should have been easy. But Stevie had no screw driver, no knife. Nothing he could use to steal a car.

He had gotten out of the car, looked back at the doorway where he had left the two men. He half hoped they had recovered enough to come after him instead of crawling away. Stevie had taken the gun from the one he had hit first. He wiped his finger-prints from the weapon and threw it over a brick wall a few feet away. He knew how to use his hands. He knew he had more trouble using his mind.

The second car he tried, a 1992 white Oldsmobile Cutlass Calais, almost renewed his faith in God. The window pushed down with pressure until he was able, just barely, to reach back and open the door. He slid into the driver's seat and tried to figure out what to do.

He opened the glove compartment searching for a tool he could use. Nothing, but there was a dark leather coin holder. He opened it. A key, a plastic Oldsmobile key.

The car turned over almost immediately and Stevie was on his way. To where? The Jockey. He wasn't sure he could trust Jake Laudano. What they had was more like an occasional business pairing than a friendship, the slow powerful big guy and the nervous little man. Neither man was quick of wit or ambitious.

Not much choice, Stevie thought. Either the Jockey or a hospital, if I can even make it to the Jockey's.

No, there was no "if" he decided as he drove. He would make it.

The next forty minutes were lost. When he woke up, the dull sunlight was coming through a window and he was lying on a lumpy sofa too small for him.

He sat up slowly. His leg was bandaged. The throbbing was tolerable. Determination was strong.

He was in a small studio apartment, sofa against one wall, a Murphy bed across the room tilted back up into the wall.

The door to the apartment suddenly opened. Stevie tried to get to his feet, but his leg sat him down again.

The Jockey came in with a paper bag in one hand.

"Brought you some coffee," he said. "And a couple doughnuts."

"Thanks," said Stevie, looking inside the bag Jake handed him and taking out the coffee.

He felt queasy. The coffee and doughnuts might help. He didn't know, didn't care. He was hungry. He picked up a doughnut and laughed.

"What's funny?" asked Jake.

"Yesterday was my birthday," said Stevie.

"No shit," said the Jockey. "Happy birthday."

Anders Kindem, Associate Professor of Linguistics at Columbia University, retained only a trace of a Norwegian accent.

Mac had read about him in a *New York Times* article. Kindem had, supposedly, definitively confirmed that whoever William Shakespeare was, he was certainly not Christopher Marlowe, Sir Walter Raleigh, or John Grisham.

Kindem, blonde straight hair, slightly gawky, with a constant smile, wasn't yet forty. He was addicted to coffee, which he drank from an oversized white mug covered with the word "words" in various colors. A tepid cup of hazelnut, which he had brewed from the tall green jar of whole beans he kept next to the grinder and coffeemaker in his office, stood next to one of four computer screens.

Kindem had two of the computers on a desk. Two others were on another desk facing the first two computers. The professor sat on a swivel chair between the four computers.

Mac sat watching him swivel, turn, move from computer to computer, looking more like a musician at an elaborate keyboard than a scientist.

Further detracting from Kindem's image as a scientist were his new-looking jeans and a green sweat shirt with rolled up sleeves. Across the front of the sweat shirt in white letters were the words YOU JUST HAVE TO KNOW WHERE TO LOOK.

Music had been playing when Mac had entered Kindem's lab, carrying a briefcase containing the disks of Louisa Cormier's novels.

Kindem had turned down the volume and said, "Detective Taylor, I deduce."

Mac shook his hand.

"Music bother you? Helps me move, think," said Kindem.

"Bach," said Mac. "Synthesizer."

"*Switched-On Bach*," Kindem confirmed.

Mac looked around the room. The computer setup used half the room. The other half contained a desk with still another computer on it and three chairs facing the computer screen. Framed degrees and awards hung on the walls.

Kindem followed the detective's eyes and said, "I hold small seminars, discussions really, with the graduate students I advise."

He nodded at the three chairs.

"Very small seminars. And the adornments on the wall? What can I say? I'm ambitious and possess a small streak of academic vanity. The disks?"

Mac found a spot at the end of one of the desks holding two computers. He opened his briefcase, took out the disks, each in a marked sleeve, and handed them to Kindem.

"You'll want to read them," Mac said. "You can give me a call when you know something."

Mac handed Kindem a card. Kindem had placed the disks between two of the computers. "Don't have to read them," Kindem said. "Don't want to read them, certainly not on a computer screen. I spend enough time reading things on screens. When I read a book, I want it in my hands and on a page."

Mac agreed, but said nothing.

Kindem was smiling.

"I can tell you some things quickly," he said. "If your questions are simple. If you want a full analysis, give me a day. I'll have one of my grad students prepare and print out or E-mail you a report."

"Sounds fine," said Mac.

"Okay," said Kindem loading each disk into a tower between two computers.

Each of the six disks went in with a whir and a click.

"So," he said. "What am I looking for?"

"I want to know if the same person wrote all these books," said Mac.

"And?" asked Kindem.

"Whatever else you can tell me about the author," said Mac.

Kindem went to work displaying his keyboard virtuosity, turning up the volume of the CD he was playing, looking even more like a musician playing along with the music.

"Words, easy," said Kindem as he punched instructions moving from one computer to the next. "But don't tell my department chair. He thinks its hard. He pretends to understand it. I never call him on his encyclopedic misinformation. Words, easy. Music is harder. Give me two pieces of music and I can program them, feed them into the computer, and tell you if the same person wrote them. Did you know Mozart stole from Bach?"

"No," said Mac.

"Because he didn't," said Kindem. "I proved it for a supposed scholar who had worked the academic scam for a full professorship in Leipzig."

He went on for about ten minutes, talking constantly, drinking coffee, and then turned from one computer to another.

"Exclamation marks," he said. "Good place to start. I don't like them, don't use them in my articles. Almost no exclamation marks in scientific and academic writing. Shows a lack of confidence in one's words. Same is true of fiction. Author is afraid to let the words carry the impact so they want to give those words a boost. Punctuation, vocabulary, word repetition, how often adverbs, adjectives are used. Like fingerprints."

Mac nodded.

"First three books," said Kindem. "Overloaded with exclamation marks. Over two hundred and fifty of them in each book. Then, in every book after that, the exclamation marks disappear. The author has seen the light or . . ."

"We have a different author," said Mac.

"You've got it," said Kindem. "But there's a lot more. In the first three books, the word 'said' appears on an average of thirty times per book. I'll check, but the writer seems to be avoiding the word 'said,' almost certainly looking for other ways to ascribe dialogue. So, instead of 'she said,' the author writes, 'she exclaimed' or 'she gasped.' The later books average two hundred eighty-six uses of the word 'said.' Growing confidence? Not that extreme, not that soon. You want more?"

Mac nodded.

"Far more compound and longer sentences in the first three books," said Kindem, looking at the screen. "Casual reader might not be consciously aware of these things, but subconsciously . . . you'd have to go to someone in the Pysch Department."

"Anything else?"

"Everything else," said Kindem. "Vocabulary. For example, the word 'reciprocated' appears on average eleven times in each of the first three books. It appears in none of the others."

"Couldn't the change after the first three books be a decision to change style or a honing of the author's skills?"

"Not that big a change," said Kindem. "And I think I'll turn up more if you give me another few hours."

"The formula in all the books is pretty much the same," said Mac. "Woman is a widow or not yet married though she's in her mid thirties. She has or is responsible for a child who turns out to be in danger from a vengeful relative, the mafia, a serial killer. Police don't help much. Woman has to protect herself and the child. And somewhere in the last thirty pages, the woman confronts the bad guy or guys and prevails with a new man in her life who she's met along the way."

"Which means that whoever wrote those books followed the formula," said Kindem. "Not that it was the same person."

Mac was sure now. Louisa Cormier had written the first three books. Charles Lutnikov had written the rest.

But why would she shoot him, Mac thought. An argument? Over what? Money?

"You want printouts?" asked Kindem.

"E-mail," said Mac. "Address is on my card."

"Are you going to need me to testify at a trial?"

"Possibly," said Mac.

"Good," said Kindem. "I've always wanted to do that. Now back to the works of the now-exposed Louisa Cormier."

Stella sat in the car, drowsy and aching, while Danny drove. For the eighth time, Stella went over the Alberta Spanio file, which was in her lap.

She looked at the crime-scene photographs—body, bed, walls, side table. She looked at the bathroom photos—toilet, floor, tub, open window over the tub.

Something tickled at her brain. Something wrong. It felt like trying to remember the name of an actor or writer or the girl who sat next to you in a calculus class in high school. You should know, were sure it was inside you. You could go through the alphabet ten, fifteen times and not come up with the name and then, suddenly, it would be there.

She turned to the testimony of the two men who had been guarding Alberta Spanio, Taxx and the dead Collier.

Then as she continued to read, it struck her. She went back to the photographs of the bathroom, her photographs.

Collier had told Flack that he had stood in the tub to check and look out the window. If the killer came through the window, he or she had to have pushed the pile of snow blocking the window into the tub. There should have been some melted snow in the tub when Collier stepped in it. But there was no sign of moisture in the tub in Stella's photographs and no footprints from Collier's shoes, even though the bottoms of his shoes should have been wet from standing in the melted snow.

Why, she thought, had Collier lied?

Sheldon Hawkes sat at the desk next to Mac, looking at the videotape on the monitor in front of him.

"Once more," said Hawkes, leaning closer to the screen.

Mac rewound the tape and sipped coffee while Hawkes watched the twenty-minute tape again, sometimes fast-forwarding and halting.

"Let's hear the interrogation tape again."

Mac rewound the tape he had made of the interview of Jordan Breeze and played it again.

"You want to see him in his cell?" asked Mac. "My guess is it will confirm what we already know."

Hawkes stood and said, "You're right."

Mac listened while Hawkes told him what he had observed.

"Sure," said Mathew Drietch.

He was wiry, about forty, with sparse yellow hair and a boxer's face. He had answered Aiden Burn's request to see the .22 Louisa Cormier had used for target practice on the firing range, which was just outside the door to the office in which they now sat.

"You like the sound of gunfire?" Drietch asked.

"Not particularly," she said.

"I do," he said, looking past her at the glass-paneled door through which he could see the stations of the hand gun range. "The crack, the power. You know what I mean?"

"Not really," said Aiden. "Now, can you show me the gun?"

He got up slowly, hitching up his black denim slacks.

"When was Louisa Cormier last here?" she asked.

"A few days ago," he said. "Day before the storm I think. I can check."

He went to the door of his office, opening it to the cracking sound of gunfire. He held it open for her, then stepped out in front of her, and crossed behind the five people at the small-arms firing range.

"Cold brings them out," Drietch said. "They get a little stir-crazy and want to shoot something. This gets it out of their system."

Aiden made no response. Drietch went to a door next to the check-in desk. A man, stocky, balding, reached under the desk, pushed a button, and the door opened.

"I've got a key," said Drietch, "but Dave's almost always here."

The room was small, bright, with small wooden boxes on shelves from floor to ceiling and a small table with no chairs in the middle of the room.

"We've got almost four hundred handguns in here," said Drietch, moving to one of the shelves as he pulled a ring of keys from his pocket. "Master key opens them all."

He pulled down a box and placed it on the table in front of Aiden. Aiden looked at the box and then at the shelves.

"Some of the boxes have padlocks. Some don't," she said.

"No gun in the box, no lock," he explained.

"This box has no lock," she said, looking at the box on the table.

"Must have forgotten to put it back on," he said. "It's probably in the box."

Aiden concluded that Drietch ran a very loose ship.

"Ammunition's in a safe," Drietch said, reading her look of disapproval.

Aiden said nothing. She reached down and lifted the lid of the metal box. There was a gun inside, a Walther .22 exactly like the one Louisa had in the drawer of her desk.

"Target gun," said Drietch.

"It can still kill," said Aiden, inserting a pencil in the barrel and lifting the gun from the box.

It took her a few seconds to determine that the gun had been cleaned recently.

"Did Louisa Cormier clean this gun?"

"No, Dave does that," he said.

Aiden bagged the gun and turned to Drietch.

"I'll need a receipt for that," he said.

She took out her notebook, wrote a receipt, signed it, and handed it to him.

"Does Ms. Cormier open the box and get the gun herself?"

"No," he said. "Stands and waits. I've got the key. I take it out, check to be sure it isn't loaded, hand it to her. I bring the ammunition to her at the range. When she's done shooting, she gives the gun back and I lock it up."

"She never touches the lock or the drawer?" asked Aiden.

"She doesn't have a key," he said patiently.

Aiden nodded and checked for prints on the box. She lifted four clean ones.

Aiden put her gloves into her kit. She'd have to

check the toilets, garbage cans, trash containers outside for the missing lock. It wouldn't be fun, but it would beat digging for that bullet in the elevator pit.

The search took twenty minutes, during which time she also checked and double-checked the pay parking lot next door.

When she went back inside, Drietch was standing next to an open stall on the range, a gun resting on the platform against which he was leaning. He pointed at the gun.

As she approached, he stepped back, giving her space.

Aiden fired. The targets, familiar black on white circles, were about twenty feet away. She got off five rounds and handed him the gun. Something on the floor of the range caught her eye.

Drietch looked at the target. The pattern was all inside the bull's-eye. Aiden could have done almost as well if the targets were twice the distance away.

"You're good," he said with respect.

"Thanks," she said. "Have everyone stop firing and tell them to put their guns down."

"Why the—?" he began.

"Because there's a lock out there," she said. "And I'm going to go bag it as evidence."

"Everything is arranged," said Arthur Greenberg.

Mac had called him to double-check.

"Snow, rain, anything but the terrible Wrath of God will not stop us from going ahead," Greenberg continued. "Is there anyone you want notified?"

"No," Mac said.

He was waiting at the courthouse for a homicide detective named Martin Witz and an assistant DA named Ellen Carasco to come out of the chambers of Judge Meriman's office, hopefully with a warrant to search the apartment of Louisa Cormier.

"Then," said Greenberg, "we'll see you at ten tomorrow morning?"

"Yes," said Mac, looking at the solid door with the name of Judge Meriman engraved impressively on polished brass.

Greenberg hung up. So did Mac as the door to Judge Meriman's chamber opened and Ellen stepped out.

"He wants to talk to you," she said.

Carasco was deceptively lean. Mac knew that beneath her loose-fitting suit were the impressive muscles of a bodybuilder. Carasco was ranked among the top thirty female bodybuilders in the world in her division. Her face was clear, pretty, her hair dark and long. Stella had more than once suggested that Carasco would not turn him down if Mac were to ask her out to dinner. Mac had never followed up on the suggestion. He didn't plan to.

Mac followed her back into the judge's chamber where Detective Martin Witz sat heavily in a reddish-brown leather chair facing the judge behind the desk.

Meriman, nearing retirement, proud of his mane of white hair and his well-groomed signature white mustache, nodded at Mac, who nodded back.

"We've been over the evidence," said Meriman in

a practiced baritone. "I want to go over it again with you before I make my decision."

Mac nodded again. Meriman held out a palm indicating that Mac should sit. He sat upright in a chair identical to the one Witz was in. Carasco stood between the two seated men.

"Victim was Charles Lutnikov," said Mac. "Lived in the same building with Louisa Cormier. They knew each other."

"How well?" asked the judge.

"From the evidence, reasonably well," said Mac.

Mac told the judge about Aiden Burn's discovery of the lock that had been used on the box that held the firing range gun, the recovery of the bullet in the elevator shaft, the typewriter ribbon and what they had found on it, the report by Kindem saying that someone other than Louisa Cormier may have written most of her novels.

"Gun been tested for a match with the bullet?" Meriman asked.

"We're doing that now," said Mac.

"Flimsy," said Meriman, folding his hands and looking up at his three visitors.

"Search warrants have been issued with less," said Carasco.

"Two pieces of information," Meriman said. "First, this is a world-famous author we are talking about, a person with resources including an attorney of high cost and great skill. Second, your evidence is largely circumstantial and without substance. Highly suggestive, I agree, but—"

Mac's cell phone vibrated insistently in his pocket. He reached for it saying, "I'm sorry, Your Honor, but this may be pertinent."

"Keep it brief," said the judge, looking at the clock on his wall, "and get off the phone if it has nothing relevant pertaining to this request for warrant."

Mac answered the phone with, "Yes."

He listened. The call lasted no more than ten seconds. He flipped the cell phone closed, pocketed it, and said, "That was CSI Investigator Burn. The lock that was cut from the box has two clear fingerprints on it, Louisa Cormier's."

"It was her gun," said the judge.

"No," said Mac. "It belonged to the range. She didn't have a key, but, according to the firing range owner, she did know where the box was."

Aiden had said something else, something Mac didn't share with the judge, although he would share it if pressed. Aiden had just told Mac that the bullet from the elevator shaft and the firing-range gun were not a match.

Why, Mac thought, had Louisa Cormier broken into Drietch's to get to a gun that was not the murder weapon? The problem, Mac concluded, was that his prime suspect was a mystery writer who knew how to make a straightforward investigation look like it was committed in the Land of Oz.

Judge Meriman swiveled his chair and looked out at the gray day threatening fresh snow. Then he swiveled back and said, "I will issue a warrant for a search of the premises of Louisa Cormier for the purpose of searching for a .22 caliber weapon for the purpose of comparison with the bullet your investigator found."

There was no way there could be a match with the weapon Louisa Cormier had shown them. Mac was certain it hadn't been fired in at least two or three days, probably much longer. The chances of there being a third .22 were very slight. If there was a third gun, the murder weapon, and he didn't rule it out, Louisa Cormier had almost certainly gotten rid of it by now. For now, however, Mac would take what he could.

"Thank you," said Mac.

"And I'll need forensic evidence that, should you find it, the weapon in question proves to have been fired. If the .22 at the firing range is not the murder weapon, you can then run gun fire tests on any .22 you find in Louisa Cormier's apartment to determine if the bullet that killed Charles Lutnikov came from that weapon."

A look of conspiratorial cooperation passed between Mac and the judge.

"If in search of the specific items indicated, you come up with further evidence that Louisa Cormier has been involved in the crime under investigation, that evidence must be discovered during a search for the gun. Is that clear?"

"Yes," said Carasco, Witz, and Taylor in chorus.

"Then it's done," said Meriman.

Meriman picked up his phone and punched a button. He told someone to come into his office.

"One more thing you should know, Your Honor,"

Carasco said. "We have a confession from another party."

The judge sat back with an irritated sigh.

"Detective Taylor believes the confession is false," Carasco added.

"When you have evidence that the confession is false, *then* I'll issue the warrant for Louisa Cormier's apartment," Meriman said. "Now leave. You've wasted enough of my time."

The three visitors left the office, hearing the click of a radio being turned on behind them.

13

"MR. MARCO HAS NOTHING TO SAY TO YOU," said Helen Grandfield when Stella and Danny entered the office with two uniformed officers behind them. "And this is private property so if you don't have a warrant—"

"This is a crime scene," said Stella.

The smell of baking bread had to be strong but Stella smelled nothing. She controlled her urge, her need to wipe her nose.

"What crime?" Helen Grandfield said, rising.

"We have evidence that strongly suggests a police officer was murdered in your corridor," said Danny.

Helen Grandfield looked at Danny and the two uniformed cops who had come in with them and then glared at Stella.

"This is bullshit," she said.

"Mrs. Contranos," Stella said.

"I use and prefer the name Grandfield," the woman said.

"Except at the door to your apartment building," said Stella. "And you were born Helen Marco. Lots of names."

Helen Grandfield tried not to glare. She failed.

"We'd like to know if any of your bakery employees didn't show up for work this morning and we'd like to interview everyone working in the bakery and we'll have to insist on talking to your father again."

The use of her real name and her relationship to Dario Marco stopped the woman who was about to launch another protest.

"You live on President Street in Brooklyn Heights. Anybody from the bakery visit you last night?" asked Stella.

"No, why?"

"Someone bled on your doorstep," said Stella. "And someone vomited." Stella felt more than a little queasy. "We can match the blood when we find the bleeder. We can match DNA in the vomit when we find the person who threw up."

The woman stood, arms at her side, quivering slightly.

"Your cooperation will be appreciated," said Stella.

"My father isn't here yet," she said. "I'll need his permission to . . ."

Stella was shaking her head "no" before the woman finished.

"Steven Guista," Stella said.

"One of our delivery-truck drivers," Helen Grandfield said, pulling herself together.

"We'd like to talk to him," said Stella.

"I don't . . ."

"He assaulted a police officer and is wanted in connection with the murder of Alberta Spanio, who was scheduled to testify today or tomorrow against your uncle," said Stella.

Helen Grandfield said nothing and then, after a deep breath, spoke very calmly.

"Steve Guista has the day off. Yesterday was his birthday. My father gave him two days off. I can give you his home address."

"We've got that," said Stella. "Now, who else isn't here today who should be here?"

"Everyone else showed up for work," said Helen.

"We'll need a list of all employee names and a room where I can talk to them one by one," said Stella.

"We don't have anyplace you can do that," said Helen.

"Fine," said Stella. "We'll do it in the bakery." Stella could stand it no longer. She fished a thick tissue out of her pocket and wiped her nose.

Jordan Breeze once again sat across from detective Mac Taylor in the interrogation room. Both men had cardboard cups of coffee in front of them.

Mac turned on the tape recorder and opened the folder in front of him. It was thicker than the last time the two men had talked.

"You didn't kill Charles Lutnikov," said Mac.

Breeze smiled and drank some coffee.

"Your hand is trembling," said Mac.

"Nervous," Breeze said.

"No," said Mac, shaking his head. "Multiple sclerosis."

"You had no right to get that information from my physician," said Breeze.

"Didn't need your physician," said Mac. "We have one of our own who observed you. Jerky eye movements. Internuclear opthalmoplegia, lack of coordination between your eyes. You stuttered when I talked to you. Noticed you had trouble picking up your coffee cup, and your hands shook. You work hard and speak slowly and distinctly to keep from slurring your speech, but you can't completely control it. You can't sit up straight. You keep slouching. When I touched your hand it was abnormally cold. And twice when you were pacing your cell you almost fell. There's no way you could have walked to the river and back in the snow."

Breeze slowly sat up.

"Are you having double vision?" asked Mac. "Muscle weakness. Jerking and twitching muscles. Facial pain. Nausea. Incontinence?"

Breeze went pale and put the paper cup on the table, trying not to spill it.

"Memory problems?" Mac went on.

"You can't get my medical records," Breeze said.

"You confessed to murder," said Mac. "We put you in jail and have the prison doctor examine you."

Breeze said nothing.

"How much time do you have before full onset?" asked Mac.

"A year, two," said Breeze.

"Have a family to take care of you?"

"No one," said Breeze, his right hand visibly trembling now.

"You never had a gun," said Mac.

Breeze didn't answer.

"We found the trunk in the locker three doors to the left of yours," said Mac. "It was filled with books autographed by Louisa Cormier. You took them out of your apartment after you heard about the murder, heard we were talking to Louisa Cormier, heard that she was a suspect."

"She signed them for me," he said. "I'm a big fan. She's going to dedicate the next book to me."

"You didn't kill Charles Lutnikov. He never harassed you."

"I did."

"Was Lutnikov carrying anything when you shot him?"

"No."

"No newspaper, books . . . ?"

"Nothing."

"Is Louisa Cormier paying your medical bills?" asked Mac.

Breeze didn't answer. He turned his head away. Mac thought he detected a hint of pain.

"We'll find out," Mac said.

"She's a good person," Breeze said.

Mac didn't answer. Finally, Jordan Breeze looked down.

"Everything I touch turns to shit," said Breeze.

"Did Louisa gave you the details about the shooting?" asked Mac.

"I think I want a lawyer now," said Breeze.

"I think that's a good idea," said Mac.

One hour later, after listening to the tape of the conversation between Mac and Jordan Breeze,

Judge Meriman issued a search warrant for the apartment of Louisa Cormier.

Louisa Cormier offered Aiden and Mac no coffee this time. She was not sullen, surly, or impolite. In fact she was cooperative and gracious, but coffee and charm were clearly not on her agenda today for the CSI duo that came bearing a search warrant.

She let them into the apartment looking a bit frayed, tired and red-eyed wearing a loose-fitting flowered dress.

"Please wait," she said once they were inside.

Mac and Aiden were under no obligation to wait for her to finish the call she made to her lawyer from the wireless phone on a delicately inlaid table just inside the doorway, but they did so anyway.

"Yes," Louisa Cormier said into the phone, her eyes avoiding the investigators. "I have it in my hand."

She looked down at the search warrant.

"Shall I read it to you? . . . All right. Please hurry."

Louisa hung up the phone. "Why are you here?" she asked. "I understand someone has confessed to killing Mr. Lutnikov."

"We don't believe him," said Mac. "His name is Jordan Breeze. You know him?"

"Slightly. My attorney will be here in fifteen minutes," she said. "I must ask you to put everything back just as you find it."

Mac nodded.

"I plan to watch," Louisa said. "Front-line research for my next book."

"You finished your latest?" asked Mac politely.

Louisa smiled and said, "Almost."

Aiden and Mac stood silently for a moment, waiting for her to continue. Louisa put a hand to her forehead and said, "It may be my last, at least for a while. As you can see, it has taken a great deal out of me. May I ask what you're looking for? I might be able to save you some time and keep my carpets clean and my privacy intact."

"Among other things, a .22 caliber pistol," said Mac. "Not the one you showed us yesterday. And a bolt cutter."

"A bolt cutter?" she asked.

"The lock on the box at the firing range where you keep a pistol was cut, probably some time yesterday."

"And the gun from the box is missing?" she asked, her eyes meeting his.

"No," said Mac.

"I'm afraid you'll have to look," Louisa said. "You won't find anything. I should take notes about how it feels to be a murder suspect. I am obviously a prime suspect aren't I?"

"Looks that way," said Mac.

"A prime suspect without motive," she added.

Neither Mac nor Aiden responded. They put on their disposable gloves and began with the entryway in which they were standing.

"They were going to kill me," Big Stevie said to Jake the Jockey.

Stevie was sitting on the sofa, sunk deep, leg hurting, thinking not about his birthday or the pain in his leg but the betrayal by Dario Marco. That's all it could be, the only explanation. Stevie was a liability. He knew what had happened to Alberta Spanio. Marco couldn't take a chance on Stevie's being picked up and talking, so he had set him up at the apartment in Brooklyn.

Stevie wouldn't have talked. He had little besides a small apartment, a job driving a bakery truck, some favorite shows on television, a bar he sort of liked hanging around in, Lilly and her mother across the hall, and Marco. Until yesterday that had been enough to make him content.

"Want some coffee, a drink, something?" asked the Jockey, himself sitting at the table in the studio apartment.

"No, thanks," said Stevie.

Stevie and the Jockey had done jobs together, mostly for the Marco family. The Jockey did most of the talking when they were together, not that he was one of those can't-stop talkers, but compared to Stevie he was Leno or Letterman.

"What're you gonna do?" asked the Jockey.

Stevie didn't want to think about his options, but he forced himself. He could gather whatever money he could, which was not all that much, maybe twenty-thousand or so if he could get it out of the bank after checking to be sure it wasn't being watched by the police. He could turn himself in, testify against Anthony and Dario Marco, maybe duck the murder charge, go into witness protection. What did he owe them now? He had given them total loyalty and they had tried to kill him.

No, even if he got a good lawyer and made a good deal, he would have to do some time. He had strangled a cop. No getting around that. Stevie was seventy-one years old plus a few hours. He'd die of old age in prison if the Marcos didn't get to him first.

Stevie could more than hold his own now, but in a few years maybe, he wouldn't be fast enough to stop a prison shank from being plunged into his back. Maybe, if he was lucky, he'd be isolated from the population, live and die in a cell.

No, there was really only one thing he could do. He could kill Dario Marco. Killing Dario had no reward other than making things even. He probably should have killed the two who had tried to trap him in the doorway of Lynn Contranos's apartment building. Maybe he did kill one of them, the one he had punched in the stomach. Maybe he was off somewhere or in a hospital dying of internal bleeding. He had broken the nose of the second guy. Stevie seemed to remember his name was Jerry. Stevie had taken the gun from Jerry and thrown it away. Maybe he should have kept it, but Stevie had never liked guns. Maybe he should also kill this Lynn Contranos. When he put it all together, there really weren't many options other than to be the last man standing.

There was a knock at the door. The Jockey stood up suddenly, looked at Stevie, looked at the door.

"Who's it?" asked Jake.

"Police."

Not many choices of places to hide. The closet or the bathroom. The Jockey pointed to the bathroom. Stevie got up. Jake whispered, "Get behind the door. Don't close it. Flush the toilet."

Stevie struggled out of the deep chair and limped toward the bathroom while Jake went to the door. He glanced behind him as he moved, checking the floor for telltale drops of blood. There were none he could see.

Stevie flushed the toilet and stood behind the open door.

"I'm opening," the Jockey said, looking back to see that Stevie was inside the bathroom.

He unzipped his pants and opened the door. Jake zipped his pants back up. The cop was alone, plain clothes, leather coat.

"Jacob Laudano?" asked the cop.

"Lloyd," the Jockey replied. "Jake Lloyd. Had it changed legal."

"Can I come in?"

Jake shrugged and said, "Sure, I got nothing to hide."

He stepped back and Don Flack entered the small apartment. One of the first things he looked at was the partially open door of the bathroom.

There were eighteen employees at Marco's Bakery in Castle Hill. They were all at work except for Steven Guista.

Stella had a list of names which she checked off as each man and woman came into the office supply room where the CSI investigators had set up.

By the time they had talked to and gotten DNA and fingerprint samples from the first nine, it was clear that every employee was either an ex-con or some kind of relation of the Marco family, or both.

Jerry Carmody was number ten. He was big, broad, about forty, going to fat, and wearing a bandage on his nose. His eyes were red and swollen.

"What happened to your nose?" Stella asked after Danny had taken a throat culture from the man.

"Accident, fell," he said.

"Fell hard," she said. "Mind if I take a look?"

"Went to the doctor this morning," said Carmody. "He set it. It's been broke before."

"You're lucky the bone didn't get driven back into your brain," Stella said. "You were hit hard."

"Like I said. I fell hard," Carmody said.

"You in Brooklyn last night?" she asked.

Carmody looked around at Danny and the uniformed cop who had brought him into the supply room.

"I live in Brooklyn," Carmody said.

"Know a Lynn Contranos?"

"No."

"We'll need some of your blood," said Stella with a cough.

"What for?"

"I think Stevie Guista did that to you," she said. "You bled on Lynn Contranos's doorstep. We've got some of that blood."

Carmody went silent.

"You do know Helen Grandfield?" asked Stella.

"Sure," he said.

"She's Lynn Contranos," said Stella.

"Yeah, so?" said Carmody without interest.

"Where is Guista?" she asked.

"Big Stevie? I don't know. Home, out getting drunk or laid. How should I know? It's his birthday. Yesterday. He's probably sleeping off a binge."

"We'll talk some more about Stevie after we match your blood to the blood on the doorstep. Roll up your sleeve."

"What if I say, 'no,' " he said.

"Investigator Messer is very gentle," said Stella. "If you don't want to do it here, we go to our lab, get a court order. Who's on duty at the lab?"

"Janowitz," said Danny evenly.

"You don't want Janowitz," Stella said.

"Janowitz the Jabber," said Danny.

Carmody rolled up his sleeve.

Ned Lyons was the twelfth employee to be led into the supply room and both Danny and Stella knew they had a bingo.

Lyons was lean, well-built, worn face older than his thirty-four years. He was also obviously walking with some pain, which he tried, without any success, to hide.

"You all right?" Stella said as Lyons sat slowly on the wooden chair at the table.

"Stomach flu," he said.

"Should you be working in a bakery with stomach flu?" she asked.

"You're right," said Lyons. "Maybe I'll tell the boss I'm sick."

"Lift your shirt please," said Stella.

Lyons looked around, sighed and lifted his shirt. The bruise on his solar plexus was about the size of a pie plate. It was already turning purple, yellow, red, and blue.

"So what does that tell you?" asked Lyons.

"What did Mr. Lyons have for dinner last night?" Stella asked Danny, who, looking at Lyons, answered, "Pepperoni, sausage, and a lot of pasta," said Danny. "Mr. Lyons likes his sauce spicy."

"How do you know what I—?" Lyons began.

"Open your mouth, Mr. Lyons," Stella ordered.

A now-confused Ned Lyons opened his mouth and Stella leaned forward to look.

When she sat back, Stella said, "Got some good news for you. We found your missing tooth."

In Louisa Cormier's third book, the killer, an outwardly mild-mannered office manager, had entered a locker in his third victim's basement by using a fourteen-inch long two-and-three-quarter-pound steel-handled bolt cutter.

Louisa had described what it felt and sounded like to cut the lock and hear it thud to the concrete floor. Louisa knew how to use a bolt cutter. The lock on the box at Drietch's firing range had been cut with a bolt cutter. An examination of the lock had made that clear. On the morning of the murder, according to doorman McGee, Louisa had gone out on her usual morning walk carrying a large Barnes and Noble cloth bag, easily large enough to conceal a bolt cutter like the one the author had described in her book.

There was no bolt cutter in the collection of objects in Louisa Cormier's memento case in her library.

No bolt cutter, no .22 caliber weapon, after thirty-two minutes of looking. What Mac did find in the bottom drawer of Louisa Cormier's desk below her computer was a bound manuscript. He placed it on the desk as Louisa Cormier protested.

"That's the draft for one of my earlier books, when I was still using a typewriter. It was never published. I've been meaning to return to it, get it in publishable condition. I'd rather you not . . ."

Louisa looked at her lawyer, Lindsey Terry, who had arrived a few minutes ago. He held up his palm indicating that his client should hold her protest.

Mac placed the manuscript on the desk, opened its thick green cover, and looked down at the top page.

"Now if you would just put it back," she said. "It has nothing to do with bolt cutters or guns."

Mac flipped the manuscript open to approximately the middle of the book and looked down at the two round holes that ran through the pages.

Mac pointed to the pages before him.

"Nothing sinister," Louisa said. "I shot the book."

Mac tilted his head to one side like a bird examining a piece of something curious that might or might not be edible.

"When I finished it," she said. "I hated it. I lived in Sidestock, Pennsylvania, at the time, working for the local newspaper, free-lancing to supplement my less than considerable wages. I read the book, thought it was a complete bomb, a waste of a year of my life. So I took it outside to the woods behind the house and shot it. I thought my potential life as a writer was over before it really got started. Pure impulse."

"But you didn't throw it away," said Mac.

"No, I did not. I didn't have to. I had gotten rid of my despair. I couldn't bring myself to get rid of the manuscript. I'm glad I didn't. The manuscript is a reminder of the fact that the muses can be fickle. And now, I actually think someday I'll be able to salvage it."

"Do you mind if we take this?" said Mac, turning to the last page of the manuscript. "We'll return it."

Louisa again looked at her lawyer, Lindsey Terry, who had stood silently at her side and said nothing. Terry was nearly ancient, had retired more than a decade earlier but had come back after concluding that he no longer had the passion he had once had for raising exotic fish. Ancient or not, Lindsey Terry was formidable. He was smart and knew how to play the age card. Mac was also sure that if charges were brought against Louisa Cormier, Lindsey Terry would step aside for another lawyer, someone with a much higher profile.

"Does that manuscript have any bearing on the crime for which you obtained a warrant to search?" the lawyer asked.

"Yes sir," said Mac. "I think it does."

"I don't want him reading it," said Louisa.

"Will it be necessary for you or anyone else to read Miss Cormier's manuscript?" the lawyer asked.

"I've become a fan over the last two days," said Mac, looking down at the open page.

"Can't you . . . ?" Louisa began, looking at the bald, freckle-headed, and clean-shaven old man at her side.

"I cannot," said Terry. "I can but warn Detective Taylor that he is engaged in a search which may well be tainted by his exceeding its conditions."

"I understand," said Mac rising.

Aiden entered the room. Before Cormier or her lawyer spotted her, Aiden gave a nod to Mac to indicate that she had found nothing.

"The name of your new novel?" asked Mac.

"The Second Chance," she said.

Aiden moved to the chair Mac had vacated and turned on the computer.

"What is she doing?" asked Louisa.

"Finding the program with your new novel," said Mac.

Aiden's fingers moved quickly from keyboard to mouse and found herself looking at the desktop page. At the right side of the page was a file titled *The Second Chance*. She clicked on it and scrolled to the bottom of the document.

"Page three hundred and six," Aiden said.

"I'm almost finished," said Louisa.

Aiden went to the hard-drive icon, clicked, opened it, and found files for Louisa Cormier's novels. She looked at Mac and shook her head.

"We're finished," said Mac, taking off his gloves and putting them in his pocket. The manuscript was under his arm, his kit in the other.

When they left the apartment, Mac looked back at Louisa Cormier and decided from what he saw that the famous author no longer thought it would be interesting to be a murder suspect.

"What's the manuscript?" Aiden asked as the elevator descended.

Mac handed it to her. Aiden opened it and looked down at the holes.

"Last page," Mac said.

Aiden flipped to the final page. By the time the elevator stopped at the lobby she had skimmed it enough to know that the words she had been looking at were exactly the same words they had found on the typewriter ribbon of Charles Lutnikov.

14

"STEVIE GUISTA," Don Flack said to Jacob Laudano, the Jockey.

From where he stood in the doorway to the apartment, Don could see the whole room and the toilet and sink behind the open bathroom door.

Don closed the door behind him.

"Haven't seen Big Stevie for months," said Jacob.

"He was at the Brevard Hotel night before last," said Flack. "So were you."

"Me, no," the Jockey said.

"You won't mind a line-up then," said Flack.

"A line-up? What the hell for?"

"To see if any of the staff at the hotel recognize you," said Don. "If they do, you move up the list to murder suspect."

"Wait a minute here," said Jake, going to the table and sitting. "I didn't murder anybody. Not night before last, not never. I've got a record, sure, but I've never murdered anyone."

"Never that we could prove," said Flack.

"Maybe I was at the Brevard," said Jake. "I go

there sometimes, drop in. Between you and me and the lamppost there's a floating card game that rents a room there sometimes."

"Night before last?" asked Don.

"No action. Went somewhere else."

"Who runs this card game?" asked Flack, moving closer to Jake who backed away.

"Who runs it? Guy named Paulie. Don't know his last name. Never did. Just 'Paulie.' "

"I want Steve Guista," said Don. "If I have to step on you to get him, I'll just be leaving a small stain on the carpet."

"I don't know where he is. I swear."

"Right," said Don. "Why would you lie?"

"Right," agreed Jake.

Don was standing in front of the little man who may well have been lowered down to Alberta Spanio's window the night before last, swung in, and stabbed her in the neck.

There was no solid evidence. No fingerprints. No witness. There was just the Jockey's acquaintance with Guista, who had rented the room, and the Jockey's size and violent background that made him a good candidate for the crime.

Don took out a card and handed it to the Jockey, who looked at it.

"Call me if Guista gets in touch with you."

"Why would he?"

"You're friends."

"I told you. We hardly know each other."

"Keep the card," said Don, leaving the apartment and closing the door behind him.

When he felt reasonably sure the detective was gone, Jake looked up and watched Big Stevie limp out of the bathroom.

"He went too easy," said Big Stevie.

"He had nothing," said Jake.

Stevie took the card from the Jockey and read it.

"He could have leaned on you harder," said Big Stevie. "I busted his ribs. He should be mad as hell."

Stevie pocketed Don Flack's card and continued, "I gotta get out of here. Check the hall. See if he's out there."

"Where you going?" asked Jake, moving to the door.

"I've got something to do before he catches up to me," said Stevie.

The Jockey went to the door, opened it, looked down the hall, and turned to Stevie saying, "I don't see him."

Stevie had come up to Jake's apartment by the back stairwell, and that's where he headed after pausing to thank the Jockey.

"Sure, wish I could do more," Jake said.

Stevie limped toward the back stairwell.

"Happy birthday," said Jake.

It was a stupid thing to say. He knew it, but he had to say something. He watched Stevie open the back stairwell door and go through it. Then Jake moved to the phone and punched in a number.

When someone answered, he said, "He just left. I think he's coming for you."

"Let me get this straight here. You want me to turn in my own brother?" asked Anthony Marco.

The wire-meshed visitor's room at Riker's Island was crowded. Marco, in a modest dark suit and pale blue tie, hands cuffed in front of him, sat behind the table, his lawyer, Donald Overby, a high-priced member of the firm of Overby, Woodruff and Cole, sat at his client's side. Overby was tall, slim, about fifty with a no-nonsense military haircut. His colleagues called him "Colonel" because that had been his rank when he worked in the JAG office in Washington during the first Gulf War. His client, in contrast, was called "Bogie" only behind his back because it was safe. He looked vaguely like Humphrey Bogart, and had the same sense of being in on the secret of human vulnerability. But Anthony had a dangerous edginess, a nervous impatient energy, which had brought him to the second day of his trial for murder.

The assistant district attorney handling the case was Carter Ward, an African-American who was statesmanlike, in his late sixties, heavy, and deep-voiced. He talked to juries slowly, carefully, and simply and handled witnesses as if he were disappointed when they seemed to be telling lies.

Ward and Stella sat across from Marco and Overby. Stella was feeling woozy. She had gulped two aspirin and a Styrofoam cup of tepid tea before they entered the cage, which, on one of the three coldest days of the year, seemed oppressively hot to her.

"This is Crime Scene Investigator Stella Bonasera," Ward said calmly. "I asked her to come to this meeting."

Which was, strictly speaking, true. Ward had

asked her to come to Riker's, but it was Stella who had suggested the plan, made refinements, and gotten it approved after she and Ward talked to the district attorney, who very much wanted Anthony Marco tied in a red bow and delivered upstate to prison. A death sentence would be nice, but given the vagaries of the system, the DA was willing to settle for whatever sentence the public would accept as long as it was long, very long.

Marco nodded at Stella. She didn't nod back. Ward opened his briefcase and took out a pad of yellow lined paper.

"We all know," said Ward, "that news of the murder of Alberta Spanio has been given prominent coverage in the media. We also know that the jury, now sequestered, was exposed to the news of the murder of our principal witness against you."

Neither Marco nor his lawyer responded, so Ward went on.

"It would be foolish to assume that the jurors will not, have not concluded that your client was behind her murder, and though the judge and you will direct them to deal only with the facts presented in the case, every juror will believe Anthony Marco did on the afternoon of September sixth of last year murder Joyce Frimkus and Larry Frimkus. Killing Alberta Spanio was a nail in your coffin."

Ward was looking at Anthony Marco, who met his gaze.

"Let's try this," Ward continued. "Whoever had her killed may well have known how much damage it could do to you. Alive and testifying, Alberta

Spanio was a hanger-on on the fringes of organized crime. Your very able counsel might have, certainly would have, attacked her credibility. But now that one of the two men who was guarding Ms. Spanio, a police officer, has been murdered, murdered inside of the bakery belonging to your brother Mr. Marco . . ."

"That murder is irrelevant," said Overby.

"Probably so, probably so," said Ward. "But I'll find a way to let the jury know about it before the judge rules it inadmissible."

"What do you want, Ward?" asked the Colonel.

"Let Investigator Bonasera tell you what she has," Ward answered.

Stella told the story of her investigation, about the Spanio murder, tracking down Guista, the evidence of Collier's murder in the bakery.

When she finished, Stella wanted to find a washroom and sit with her eyes closed, waiting for the full-fledged nausea.

"Give us enough evidence to squeeze your brother for a major felony," said Ward. "And we'll take the death penalty off the table."

Prisoner and his attorney whispered and when they were done, the Colonel said, "Murder Two, you ask for minimum sentence. Mr. Marco gets twenty-to-life, gets out in ten, maybe a lot less if you leave the door open."

"Agreed," said Ward. "If the information your client gives us is true and incriminating."

"It is," said the Colonel.

Anthony smiled at Stella, who tried to glare back

but felt a feverish heaviness around her forehead and sinuses.

"What the hell," said Anthony. "Dario screwed up, on purpose or not. Doesn't make a goddamn difference. My son-of-a-bitch brother wants to take over my business operations."

"Which are?" asked Ward.

"Private," answered Marco. "That's part of this deal if we go that way."

Ward nodded his understanding.

"My brother, Dario, is a shrewd idiot," said Marco, who shook his head. "A dwarf or a jockey through a window. What kind of stupid idea is that?"

Stella held her peace, not just because she was sick and wanted to get out of there but because she was sure that no dwarf nor Jacob the Jockey had murdered Alberta Spanio. The truth was tricky on the surface, but easy to figure out when you had the crime-scene evidence.

Ward put his pocket tape recorder on the desk and sat upright with hands folded.

Anthony Marco began to talk.

Sheldon Hawkes had received the call from Mac asking that the body of Charles Lutnikov be brought out of the vault.

When Aiden and Mac arrived, Lutnikov's naked, white body, skin flap pulled back to reveal his rapidly decaying organs, lay on the metal table that gleamed under the intense white light.

"Put the skin flap back," said Mac.

Hawkes put the skin flap back in place and Aiden

produced the manuscript with two holes they had taken from Louisa Cormier's apartment.

She held the book open for Hawkes to see. He examined the book and nodded. He knew what Mac and Aiden wanted. There were two ways to go, at least two ways. He chose to remove a canister of clear, two-foot-long plastic trajectory rods from the cabinet, extract two, and put the rest away.

Then he inserted the rods into the holes in the body. The body had gone flaccid. He had to probe gently to be sure the rods were following the path of the bullet. It took him about three minutes, after which he backed up and let Aiden approach the corpse. "Can you clip off most of the rods without moving them?" she asked. He nodded, went to a cabinet, removed a large glistening metal clipper, and snipped the rods down so they protruded about an inch out of the body. Then, with Hawkes's help, she lined up the rods with the two holes in the manuscript. It was a match. She could have pegged the book to the dead man with a little exertion, but it wasn't necessary.

"Conclusion," said Hawkes, leaning over to remove the rods. "The gun that shot Charles Lutnikov was used to make the two holes in your manuscript."

"He was holding the manuscript up in front of him when she fired," said Mac. "Bullet went through the paper, bounced out, and when it exited, dropped down the elevator shaft."

"Sounds right to me," said Hawkes.

"But," said Aiden, "do we have enough for an arrest?"

"She'll need a good story," said Hawkes.

"She's a mystery novelist," said Aiden.

"No, she's not," said Mac. "Lutnikov was the novelist."

"Back to square one and her best defense," said Aiden. "Why should she want to kill the goose that was laying best-selling novels?"

"Back to the lady," Mac said.

"Need the body anymore?" asked Hawkes.

Mac shook his head and Hawkes gently rolled the table toward the bank of drawers holding the dead.

"We still need the gun and the bolt cutter," Aiden reminded Mac as they left Hawkes laboratory. "And she's probably gotten rid of them."

"Probably," Mac agreed. "But not definitely. We have three important things on our side. First, she knows where they are. And second, she doesn't know how much we know or how much we can discover at a crime scene."

"And third?" Aiden asked.

"The bolt cutter," he said. "She used it in one of the first three novels, one she wrote. All the trophies in her library are from the first three novels. She'd probably want to keep the bolt cutter."

"Probably," said Aiden.

"Possibly," said Mac. "She doesn't know we can match a bolt cutter to whatever it cut."

"Let's hope not," she said. "Even if we find it, we still need the gun."

"One piece of evidence at a time," said Mac.

Getting away was not an option. Big Stevie knew that. He didn't have the money or the smarts for it, and both the police and Dario's people were looking for him.

The cab driver kept eyeing him in the mirror. Stevie didn't care.

Stevie had picked up the cab at a stand near Penn Station. The driver had been sitting behind the wheel reading a paperback novel. He had looked over his shoulder when Stevie closed the door and saw more than he wanted to see.

If Stevie had hailed him on the street, the driver, Omar Zumbadie, would not have picked him up.

The hulking old white man needed a shave. He needed some fresh clothes. And he reeked of something foul. Omar prayed that the old man would not throw up. He didn't look drunk, just tired and in a head-bobbing trance.

The cabbie took Riverside Drive north to the George Washington Bridge, toward the Cross Bronx Expressway. Big Stevie counted his money. He had forty-three dollars and he was bleeding again through the make-shift bandage the Jockey had wrapped tightly around his leg.

If Stevie were a vindictive man, he would have killed the detective who had come to the Jockey's apartment. It would have been easy. The detective, whose name was Don Flack, according to the card he had given to the Jockey, had shot Big Stevie. Birthday greetings from New York's finest, a bullet in the leg. The bullet wasn't there anymore, but it hurt, and the hurt was spreading. Big Stevie ignored it. It would be over soon, and, if he were lucky, which he probably wouldn't be, he'd have some money and get Dario Marco off his back.

Life was unfair, Stevie thought as the cab got off at the Castle Hill exit. Stevie accepted that, but Dario's betrayal of him by sending the two bakery hacks to kill him was beyond unfair. Stevie had been a good soldier, a good truck driver. Customers on his route liked him. He got along great with kids, even Dario's grandkids, who at the ages of nine and fourteen looked like their father and trusted no one.

Forget unfair. Now it was about making things even and maybe staying alive. The other option was calling the cop whose card he held, calling him, and imagining hours, days of grilling, betraying, putting on a suit and going to Dario's trial, being made to look like an idiot by one of Dario's lawyers. And then prison. It didn't matter how long. It would be long enough, and he was already an old man.

No, the way he was going was the only way to go.

"Mister," said Omar.

Stevie kept looking out the window. He had put the detective's card back in his pocket and now had his hand wrapped around the small painted animal Lilly had made him.

"Mister," Omar repeated, being careful to not sound in the least bit irritated.

Stevie looked up.

"We're here," said Omar.

Stevie refocused and recognized the corner where they had stopped. He grunted and reached into his pocket.

"How much?"

"Twenty dollars and sixty cents," said Omar.

Stevie reached through the slightly fogged, supposedly bulletproof slider which Omar slid open and handed the driver a twenty and a five dollar bill.

"No change," said Stevie.

Omar stared at the bills as Stevie got out of the cab. It wasn't easy. His remaining good leg had to do all the work along with his hands. But Stevie's hands were strong.

"Thanks," said Omar.

The bills in his hand both had bloody fingerprints on them, fingerprints that looked fresh.

Omar waited till Stevie had cleared the cab and shut the door before he sped away. He placed the two bills on top of the paperback novel in the seat next to him.

The smart thing to do, Omar thought, was to clean the bills as best he could and forget the big man. He was sure most drivers would do that, but Omar had seen blood on men's hands in Somalia, and in Somalia there had been almost no one willing to stand up and denounce the slayers of women and children, and there had been, really, no one to denounce them to. To seek justice, he thought as he drove, one risked his own and his family's death.

But this was America. He was here legally. Things were not perfect, not always safe especially for a cab driver.

Omar was a good Muslim. He did what he was sure a good Muslim should do. He reached for his cab radio and called the dispatcher.

* * *

"Were your shoes on or off?" asked Stella, sitting with eyes closed behind the desk, a cup of black coffee in front of her. She held the phone to her left ear, her right hand on the coffee cup. She had a chill.

"Off," Ed Taxx said into the phone in his living room. "We had just gotten up, pulled on our pants and shirts and socks."

"You're sure?" asked Stella.

"Are you all right?" asked Taxx.

Everyone was asking her that now.

"I'm fine," she said. "Thanks."

"That's it?" Taxx asked. "That's all you want to know?"

"For now," said Stella.

"Fine," said Taxx. "Take fifteen aspirin and call me in the morning."

"I will," said Stella flatly.

"I was joking," said Taxx.

"I know," said Stella, "but it was almost good advice anyway."

She hung up the phone.

15

NOAH PEASE, Louisa Cormier's new high-profile lawyer, reminded Mac of one of Edgar Lee Masters's *Spoon River* characters, clean-shaven and imperially slim.

Pease was about fifty, roughly good-looking with a deep voice that, in addition to his record representing high-profile corporate figures, athletes, and actors in criminal cases, made him perfect for Court TV.

Next to Pease, lean, nattily dressed in a well-pressed suit, on the sofa, her back to the window with the broad panoramic view of the city, sat Louisa Cormier. Across from them sat Mac Taylor and Joelle Fineberg, a green-suited petite woman, who had been with the District Attorney's office for a little over a year. She looked as if she was young enough for a Sweet Sixteen party.

The total practical legal experience in Louisa Cormier's living room was twenty-seven years. One of those years belonged to Joelle Fineberg.

"You realize, Ms. Fineberg," said Pease slowly, "Ms. Cormier is cooperating fully. At this point there is nothing that compels her to talk to you unless you are prepared to bring charges."

"I understand," said Fineberg, her voice and smile indicating that she appreciated the cooperation.

"No one knows about your investigation or that of the police and . . ." Pease said, looking at Mac. "Your Crime Scene unit. Detective Taylor's accusation that my client didn't write her own books cannot be made public. If it is, in any way, we shall bring suit against the City of New York and Detective Taylor for eighteen million dollars. And I'm confident we can get that figure. You understand what I'm saying?"

"Perfectly," said Fineberg, hands folded atop the briefcase in her lap. "Your client is more interested in her reputation than in the fact that we are building a murder charge against her."

"My client murdered no one," said Pease.

Louisa, obviously under orders from her attorney, said nothing, didn't react to Fineberg's accusation.

"We believe she did," said Fineberg.

"Fine," said Pease. "Let's go over your evidence. A tenant of this building is shot and killed by a .22 caliber weapon. No weapon found. No witnesses. No fingerprints. No DNA evidence."

"The dead man ghost-wrote your client's novels," said Fineberg. "He has two bullet holes in him that left holes in the manuscript he was carrying and that Detective Taylor and his people found in this apartment."

Pease nodded.

"Let's suppose," said Pease, "and it's just supposition mind you, the first explanation that pops into my head. The gun belongs to Mr. Lutnikov or someone who is on the elevator with him. The two people have a fight. The other person shoots Mr. Lutnikov and gets away. Mr. Lutnikov, now dead, goes up to this floor. He or his murderer had hit the button. My client has been waiting for him to deliver the manuscript. The elevator door opens and she sees Lutnikov dead, manuscript clutched to his chest. Horrified but desperate she takes the manuscript after being certain the poor man is dead and sends the elevator back down to the lobby where she knows it will be discovered. Bad judgment, perhaps, but a jury would sympathize and, let me remind you, you have no murder weapon."

"I'm innocent," Louisa Cormier said suddenly.

There was no sign of indignation nor an appeal for sympathy in her words. They were simply stated.

Pease touched his client's shoulder and looked at Joelle Fineberg. "And remember, that is only the first possible scenario I could think of," said Pease.

Both Fineberg and Mac didn't doubt that.

"We have enough to take to a grand jury," Fineberg said.

Pease shrugged.

"Publicity, trial, loss for the District Attorney's office, and a lawsuit on behalf of my client," he said. "My client did not kill Charles Lutnikov nor did he ghost-write her books. The manuscript Charles Lutnikov copied from my client's original and most recent novel was a one-time favor to a fan who had been quietly harassing Ms. Cormier for years."

"So," said Fineberg. "She gave him a printout of a completed book so he could copy it?"

"No," said Pease. "So he could read it before anyone else. She had no idea he was copying it until he called her and told her. She insisted that he bring his copied manuscript to her, which he did. He was clutching it close to his chest when he was shot by whoever shot him."

"That's what happened," said Louisa.

"You told us yesterday that you were still writing the book," Mac said.

"Re-writing," Louisa said. "You misunderstood. I was working on the second draft."

"May I ask you a question?" asked Mac.

Louisa looked at Pease who said, "You may ask, but I may tell my client to decline to answer. We want to cooperate with the police, to help find Mr. Lutnikov's murderer."

Fineberg was not surprised by Mac's question. He had proposed it to her on the way to the apartment.

"Can you define any of the following words?"

Mac had removed the small notebook from his pocket.

"Mufti, obsequious, tendentious."

Louisa Cormier blinked.

"I don't . . ." she began.

"Those words appear in your books," said Mac. "I've got seventeen others I'd like to ask you about."

"Do you use a thesaurus, Louisa?" asked Pease calmly.

"Sometimes," she answered.

Pease raised his hands and smiled.

"And our expert witness who'll testify that Charles Lutnikov wrote Louisa Cormier's novels?" asked Fineberg.

"I've got five expert witnesses who will say she did write her own books," said Pease. "All with Ph.D.'s. Where do we go from here?"

"We find the murder weapon," said Mac. "And the bolt cutter your client used to open the lock at Drietch's firing range."

"Good luck," said Pease. "According to your own report, the gun found in the box at the firing range is not the one used to kill Mr. Lutnikov."

"It's not," said Mac, his eyes on Louisa, "but I think I know where the one that did kill Lutnikov is."

"And the elusive bolt cutter?" asked Pease.

Mac nodded.

"A bluff," said Pease. "Where are they?"

"Right out in the open," said Mac. "That sound familiar Ms. Cormier?"

Louisa Cormier shifted slightly and did not return his look.

"I think we're finished here," said Pease. "Unless you are prepared to arrest my client."

Joelle Fineberg rose. So did Mac and Pease. Louisa Cormier remained seated, her eyes fixed on Mac.

In the elevator going down, Joelle Fineberg said, "'Right out in the open?' Where did you get that, Poe or Conan Doyle?"

"From one of the Louisa Cormier novels," said Mac. "I don't know where she got it."

The elevator arrived at the lobby and the doors opened.

"Call me when you have something," she said.

Mac nodded.

In the lobby they passed McGee, the doorman, who nodded and smiled. It was snowing again, not much, but it was snowing. The temperature had dropped to five above zero.

"The gun is in this building," said Mac. "She can't get rid of it."

"Why?"

"Because we know she owns it," he said.

"You examined her gun," said Fineberg. "It hasn't been fired."

"The gun she showed us hadn't been fired," he corrected.

It was the lawyer's turn to nod.

"And the bolt cutter?" asked Joelle Fineberg. "What if she did get rid of it?"

"She thinks she's smart enough to pull it off."

"What?"

Mac smiled and walked toward the stairwell. Joelle watched him for a few moments and then buttoned her coat, wrapped her scarf around her neck, and put on a pair of dark earmuffs she took out of her pocket.

When she looked back over her shoulder, Mac was no longer in sight. McGee opened the door for her and she stepped out into the bitter, biting cold.

"Where did you get this?" asked Hawkes.

"Tissue in the garbage," answered Danny. They

were sitting in the tile-floored box of a room in the basement of CSI headquarters where the coffee-, soda-, sandwich-, and candy-dispensing machines lined the walls like slot machines in Las Vegas washrooms. Above them, one of the bank of florescent lights sputtered softly.

Sheldon Hawkes put his tuna fish sandwich with too much mayo on the paper plate in front of him and took the slide from Danny.

"Come up and take a look at it under the microscope," said Danny.

"You've identified it?" asked Hawkes, handing the slide back and picking up his sandwich.

"Rare, but not all that rare," said Danny.

"You tell anyone?"

"No one around," said Danny. "Stella called. She said she was on her way in, asked me to have all the Spanio crime-scene photographs out."

"How did she sound?"

"Sick," said Danny.

Hawkes finished his sandwich, downed the last of his Diet Dr Pepper, threw his trash away, and got up.

"Let's take a look," he said.

On the table in front of Stella were neatly arranged photographs of the bedroom in which Alberta Spanio was murdered and the bathroom adjacent to it. It was the bathroom in which she was interested right now.

She selected four photographs and scanned them, her head bent close to each image. Her recollection proved to be right. Leaning over increased the pain in her head and the threat in her stomach.

Stella reached for the tea she had been trying to sip in the hope of it settling her stomach. The tea was not inviting. She changed her mind.

She was sure she was right. She was reasonably sure she knew what had happened and who had killed Alberta Spanio and maybe even why Collier had been murdered. If it weren't for the flu, which she now acknowledged, she would have figured it out much sooner.

Someone came through the laboratory door behind her. Stella stood up and turned. She felt light-headed but determined.

Hawkes came in with Danny.

"I figured it out," she said, wondering what Hawkes was doing here. He seldom left his corpses except to eat and go home.

"What?" asked Danny, approaching with Hawkes at his side.

"The Spanio murder," she said.

"Great," said Danny.

"I've got to call Mac," said Stella.

"I've got some slides I want you to look at right away," said Danny.

Hawkes held up two slides.

"Can't it . . . ?"

Hawkes was shaking his head, "no."

"What's going on here?" she asked.

"Look at the slides," said Danny.

Stella sighed and moved to a microscope, switching on the light and taking the slides from Danny. She sat down, the two men looming behind her. She adjusted the focus on the first slide. The microscope was multifunctional and powerful. With a few adjustments, she had the slides lined up next to each other so they could be compared.

"Virus," she said. "Same on both plates."

"You know what it is?" asked Hawkes.

"Don't recognize it," said Stella.

"It's leptospirosis," said Hawkes.

Stella blinked, going through the catalogue of diseases in her mind.

"It's rare," Stella said.

"One to two hundred cases a year in the United States," said Danny. "Half of those in Hawaii. It's a tropical-climate disease normally."

"We have an exception," said Hawkes. "What do you know about the disease?"

"Bacterial infection usually caught from animal urine," she said. "One of our cases? Lutnikov, Spanio, Collier, one of Dario Marco's men?"

"No," said Hawkes. "It's you. Danny got a sample of your mucus from a tissue you threw away. You don't have the flu. What do you know about leptospirosis?"

"Next to nothing," said Stella, leaning back and closing her eyes.

Hawke's hand touched her forehead.

"Fever," he said. "Headache?"

"Yes."

"Chills, muscle ache, vomiting?"

"Nausea, no vomiting."

Hawkes gently turned her in the chair and looked at her face.

"Slight jaundice, red eyes," he said.

"You sound like you're doing an autopsy," Stella said.

"My patients don't usually talk back," he said. "Abdominal pain, diarrhea?"

"A little of both," Stella said.

"Hospital," said Hawkes.

"How about outpatient treatment?" she asked. "I'm really close on the Spanio murder."

"Danny can follow through. You know what untreated or improperly treated leptospirosis can turn into? Kidney damage, meningitis, liver failure. I've seen one death from it. When did you start showing symptoms?"

"Yesterday," Stella said, resigned. "Maybe the day before."

"You remember being exposed to animal . . . ?" Hawkes began.

"The cats," said Danny.

"What was that?" asked Hawkes.

"Old woman died in her home on the East Side," said Stella. "Cat woman, forty-seven we could find. We ran it as a crime scene because there were signs that someone had broken into the house, but she had a heart attack. Overweight, seventy-eight years old. Didn't take care of herself."

"Or her cats," said Hawkes. "Where are they now?"

"Humane society took them," said Danny.

Hawkes shook his head.

"See if you can round them up," Stella said to Danny.

"If there are any recently dead ones," Hawkes said, "I'd like to have them brought in."

"My guess," said Stella, "is that, except for a lucky few, they were all euthanised and cremated. Treatment?"

"Overnight in a hospital bed," said Hawkes. "Antibiotics, probably doxycycline. I'll call Kirkbaum and have a room saved for you."

"How long?" asked Stella.

"If we caught it early enough, two or three days. If not, we could be talking a week or two. Judging from the viral load, it may just be that Danny saved your life."

Danny grinned smugly and adjusted his glasses.

"I'm a stubborn ass," she said. "Thanks."

"You're welcome," said Danny. "And, yes, you are one major stubborn ass."

Stella stood and said, "Danny, gather all these Spanio photos and tell Mac to come to the hospital as soon as he can get there."

"You'll be all right," said Hawkes. "I haven't had a complaint from a patient yet."

"That's because they're all dead," said Stella.

There was a uniformed cop at the entrance to Marco's Bakery and another uniformed cop at the back exit on the shipping dock. This didn't surprise Big Stevie.

The only question was: Were the cops there to keep Marco from getting out, or to keep Stevie or someone else from getting in?

It didn't matter. Stevie knew at least two other ways into the building. He knew that the window to the men's toilet was easy to open. Even if it was locked, the lock was just a small slide bolt he would have no trouble breaking with a firm tug. He wouldn't even make much noise.

The problem with going through the toilet window was that he would have to find something to stand on, get leverage, and then climb through. Usually this would be no problem. But with his leg growing ever more numb, the task might be more than he could handle. Once inside the toilet he would have to go out the door past the bakers and their assistants. He was a familiar sight back there, at least normally. Normally, no one would have paid much, if any, attention to the big man, but today might be altogether different. He doubted that even in his weakened state, bleeding and walking like a mummy in those old movies, that anyone in the bakery would be able to stop him and most would probably simply pretend they had never even noticed him. They had all done time. D and D. Deaf and dumb. It was the stay alive philosophy of prison.

No, it would have to be the storage basement. He didn't know if any of the opaque windows could be opened without making noise that would attract attention. He did know that he wasn't seen by the cop on the loading dock. Window number one was firm, didn't budge, probably hadn't been opened in twenty years or more. Window number two had four sections. The dirty glass plate in the upper right-hand section of the window was loose and the window itself had a little give to it.

Stevie found a small chunk of concrete and knelt by the ground-level window. He tore off a piece of his undershirt, placed it against the loose pane, and struck the cloth with the piece of concrete, struck it gently. There wasn't much noise, but the pane did not give way. He tried again, striking a little harder. Something cracked. There was now a hole in the glass about the size of his fist. He put down the concrete and took the torn piece of shirt from the window.

Stevie inched his thick fingers through the hole in the glass. He felt the cutting of the glass, ignored it and slowly worked the top piece of glass loose. He placed it on the ground.

He wiped his bleeding fingers on his already bloody pants and reached through the open space in the window. There was just enough room for him to force his hand and arm far enough to reach the lock. It was rusted shut, but Stevie was determined. He shoved. The rusted metal bolt came off. Using his right arm, sitting awkwardly, he reached in and put pressure on the window. The window resisted. Slowly Stevie began to feel the window losing the battle. Suddenly, the entire window shot up on creaking hinges.

Stevie knelt panting, waiting, listening for running footsteps, but none came.

He had finished the easy part of his task. Now came the hard part, getting his bulk through the open window. He knew it would be close. He took off his coat and placed it on the ground.

A cold wind drove through him and he realized

that snow was falling again. He was growing weaker and he would have to move quickly while he was still able.

He eased his injured leg through the open window followed by his good one and started to push himself backward through the window. When he was inside as far as his stomach, it felt tight, but not impossibly tight. He kept pushing backward. His stomach scraped against the thin metal frame of the window, and he wasn't sure if he would make it through. He was sure at this point that he would never be able to pull himself back out. He struggled, grunting, seeing the blood from his fingers against the snow and then, suddenly, he popped through the window and went sprawling backward into dusty darkness.

He lay on his back panting, out of breath, eyes closed. Big Stevie was in pain. He was cold. And he was bloody. But he was on a mission, and he was inside Marco's Bakery.

The search perimeter around Drietch's firing range had been widened. Two uniformed officers were helping Aiden search for the missing bolt cutter.

Aiden was sure that Louisa Cormier had simply cut the lock, wiped off her fingerprints, and thrown it on the firing range. Why hadn't she done the same thing with the bolt cutter or dropped it and the lock in the garbage?

They should have found it by now.

Her phone vibrated in her pocket and she answered it.

"Come into the lab," Mac said. "I found the bolt cutter."

"Where?"

"Basement of Louisa Cormier's building," he said. "She had it lined up with other tools. Building maintenance man has a bolt cutter but he said this one isn't it."

"She hid it in plain sight," Aiden said.

"Right out of her fourth novel," Mac said. "Or should I say right out of Charles Lutnikov's first Louisa Cormier novel, only in that one it was a shovel."

"Prints?"

"One," said Mac. "Partial. Good enough for a positive identification. It's Louisa Cormier's."

"I'll be right there," said Aiden, closing her cell phone and going in search of the two uniformed officers who were combing the area.

"I'm on my way to the hospital," he said.

"Right," said Aiden, who wasn't certain how she felt about confronting Louisa Cormier again. Aiden wasn't sure if the woman was cunning and manipulative or if she had simply been caught in a nightmare. Aiden Burn wasn't ready to bet on either.

16

A WHITE, SAND-PEBBLED BEACH hovered over Stella when she opened her eyes. She could even hear the rhythmic beating of something that may have been surf.

Stella hadn't had a vacation in, what was it, three years. She had never wanted one, had never wanted to get away. There was always a new case or one half finished.

The web of first waking passed in a second or two and she realized that the pebbled beach was the ceiling and the sound of the surf was a monitor whose thin tentacles adhered to her body.

Stella's mouth was dry.

She turned her head and saw Mac standing to her left.

"How . . . ?" she started to say, but it came out as a painful incoherent crackle.

She coughed painfully and pointed at a white plastic pitcher and a glass on the table next to the bed. Mac nodded, poured water, removed the wrapping from a straw, and inserted it in the glass.

"Slow," said Mac, holding the glass for her to drink.

The first sip burned. She had a slight retching sensation, but it passed and she drank some more.

"How bad is it?" she asked.

"You'll be fine," Mac said. "You blacked out. Danny and Hawkes brought you here. Hawkes's friend got you started on glucose and antibiotics. He found an expert on leptospirosis in Honolulu, called him and . . . here you are."

"How long will I be here?"

"A few days. Then a few days at home," said Mac. "If you'd had a culture when you first started to get sick, you wouldn't have to be here."

"I'm a workaholic," she said with what she hoped was a smile.

Mac returned the smile. Stella looked around the hospital room. There wasn't much to see. A window to her left and one in a corner looked out at a red building across the street. On the wall was the reproduction of a painting she thought she recognized, three women in peasant dresses in a field, stacks of hay behind them. The women were leaning over to pick up something—beans, rice—and drop it in baskets on the ground.

Mac followed her eyes.

"Woman on the right," said Stella. "She's in pain. Look at the deformed C-shaped curve of her back from years of bending. When she stood up, she'd be in pain and bent over. She's not far from being unable to bend like that."

"You want to run some tests on her?" asked Mac.

"Not unless someone kills her or she kills someone else," said Stella, still looking at the painting. "How old do you think the original painting is?"

"Jean François Millet," said Mac. "The painting's called *The Gleaners*, 1857."

Stella turned to look at him and said nothing.

"My wife had some prints of his work," said Mac. "One of the highlights of our trip to Europe was to see Millet's *Angelius* in the Musée d'Orsay."

Stella nodded. It was more information about Mac's dead wife than he had ever given up before.

Mac's smile was broader now.

"She saw beauty in that painting," he said. "And you see a woman with a medical condition."

"I'm sorry," said Stella.

"No," said Mac. "You're both right."

"Mac," she said. "I know who killed Alberta Spanio, and it wasn't the Jockey."

When Don Flack answered his cell phone, Mac told him what Stella had said.

"I'll go right there," said Flack.

"You want backup?" asked Mac.

"I won't need it."

"Anything new on Guista?"

"I'll find him," said Flack, touching the tender area of his broken ribs.

Flack closed his cell phone and kept driving, but instead of heading for Marco's Bakery, he now headed for Flushing, Queens.

The temperature was up to fifteen degrees and the snow had stopped. Traffic moved slowly, and after almost four days of frigid snowstorm tempers were on edge. Road rage at a snail's pace was ever ready to break out.

Don checked his watch. The phone rang. It was Mac again.

"Where are you?" Mac asked.

Don told him.

"Pick up Danny at the lab. He has the crime-scene photographs and Stella just briefed him," said Mac.

"Right," said Flack. "How is she doing?"

"Fine, doctors say she'll be back at work in a few days."

"Tell her I asked," said Don, signing off again.

Danny was waiting behind the glass doors wearing a thick knee-length down coat and a hat with flaps that covered his ears. He held a briefcase in one gloved hand and waved at Don with the other to let him know he was coming out.

As soon as he opened the door, his glasses clouded and he had to pause to wipe them with his scarf.

"Cold," he said, getting into the heated car.

"Cold," Flack agreed.

Danny Messer told Flack everything that Stella had told him on the phone as they drove to Flushing. Flack looked for holes, alternatives to Stella's conclusions, but he couldn't come up with any. He turned on the radio and listened to the news until they pulled up in front of Ed Taxx's house.

Taxx answered the door. He was wearing jeans and an open-collared white shirt with a brown wool sweater. He had a cup of coffee in his hand. The word DAD was in bright red with a blue border.

"Anyone else home?" asked Don.

A television set was on somewhere in the house. A woman in some show was laughing. The laughter sounded insincere to Don.

"All alone and getting bored," said Taxx, stepping back to let the two men in and closing the door behind them. "I'm still on leave till the department finishes its investigation."

Taxx led the way into the living room, asking over his shoulder if he could get either of them some coffee or a Diet Coke. Both men declined.

Taxx sat in an overstuffed chair and Don and Danny on the sofa.

"What brings you here?" asked Taxx, taking a sip of coffee.

"A few questions," said Flack.

"Shoot."

"When you knocked down the door to Alberta Spanio's bedroom, you immediately went to the bed?"

"Right," said Taxx.

"And you sent Collier to the bathroom?" Flack continued.

"I wouldn't say I sent him. We just did what we had to. What . . . ?"

"Collier said you told him to check the bathroom," said Flack.

"Probably," Taxx agreed.

"Did you go into the bathroom after he came out?"

Taxx thought and then answered, "No. We went into the living room and called in the murder.

Neither of us went back in the room. It was a crime scene."

"Collier said he stood in the tub and looked out the open window," said Flack.

"I wasn't in there with him," said Taxx, looking puzzled.

"Danny, show him the photographs," said Flack.

Danny opened the briefcase and took out the stack of crime-scene photographs he and Stella had taken. He selected four of them and handed them to Taxx. All four photographs were of the bathtub and the open window. Taxx looked at the photographs and then handed them back to Danny.

"What am I supposed to be seeing in those pictures?" Taxx asked, putting down his coffee mug.

"There's no snow, no sign of snow or ice in the tub," said Flack. "It was too cold in that room for the snow to melt."

"So?" asked Taxx.

"If someone came through the window to kill Alberta Spanio, he'd have to push in the snow that had piled up against the window."

Taxx nodded.

"Maybe he swept the snow out with his arm or leg instead of pushing it in," said Taxx.

"Why?" asked Danny. "Why let go with one hand or reach in with a foot and pull the snow back outside. It wouldn't help cover the crime. The window was open. It makes no sense to do anything except swing through the window, pushing or kicking the snow in, climb in and out of the tub, murder Spanio and go out the way he came in."

"Someone inside the bathroom pushed the snow out," said Flack.

"Why? And who? Collier? Alberta?" asked Taxx.

"Alberta Spanio was knocked out from an overdose of sleeping pills," said Danny, "and even if she weren't, why open a window to let in zero-degree air and snow?"

"Collier?" asked Taxx.

"We think whoever killed Alberta Spanio pushed that snow out, wanting us to think someone had come through the window," said Flack. "Because if the murder wasn't committed by someone coming through the window, that leaves only two possible suspects."

Taxx said nothing. His tongue pressed against the inside of his right cheek.

"Collier?" he repeated.

"When and how?" asked Danny. "The door to the bedroom was locked all night."

"And the bathroom window was closed," Taxx reminded them. "Both Collier and I confirmed that. We left the bedroom together."

"But in the morning you broke down the door and one of you went to Spanio's bedside while the other went to the bathroom," said Danny. "That was the only time Spanio could have been murdered. You were the one who went to the bed, pulled the knife out of your pocket, and stabbed the unconscious Spanio in the neck. You could have done it in five seconds. A CSI investigator timed it."

"The woman," said Taxx, looking out the window.

"Stella figured it out," confirmed Don.

"Dario Marco hired Guista and Jake Laudano to get that room at the Brevard Hotel," said Flack. "They were supposed to be seen, a big strong man and a tiny one. We were supposed to think they had murdered Spanio so the real killer, you, wouldn't be suspected."

"Guista was there to pull the window to the washroom up by dangling a chain down and hooking it onto the hoop you had screwed into the bathroom window."

"Far-fetched," said Taxx.

"Maybe," Flack agreed, "but we're pulling Jake Laudano in and when we have both him and Guista, the DA starts dealing and they start talking."

"Am I under arrest?" Taxx asked softly.

"You are about to be," said Flack.

"I think I should call a lawyer," said Taxx.

"Sounds like the thing to do," said Flack.

The detective rose with a sudden sharp sting from the broken ribs in his chest. He took the four steps to Taxx and handcuffed the man's hands behind his back.

Don adjusted his glasses and put the photographs away while Flack began the Miranda. Don said the words slowly, and for some reason it sounded like a well-memorized prayer.

Aiden examined the bolt cutter and the broken lock. She had done a magnified close-up photograph of both the edges of the bolt cutter and the ridges and scars where the lock had been cut.

She sat in the lab now comparing the two.

The small ridges of the blade were almost invisible
to the naked eye, but close up they were as good as
fingerprints. There was no doubt in her mind. There
would be no doubt in the minds of jurors. The lock
Aiden had found at the firing range had been cut by
the bolt cutter Mac had found in the basement of
Louisa Cormier's apartment building.

She picked up the phone, called Mac and told him
what she had found.

"It's enough," said Mac.

"Enough for . . . ?" she said, letting the question
hang.

"An arrest," said Mac. "I'll meet you at Louisa
Cormier's with someone from homicide."

Aiden hung up. All the evidence against Louisa
Cormier was circumstantial. There were no eyewit-
nesses and they had not found the smoking gun. But
most cases were won in court with a preponderance
of compelling circumstantial evidence. Smart defense lawyers could attack it all, create alternative
scenarios, explain mistakes, confuse the issue, but
Aiden, who was on her feet and heading for her
coat, didn't think any obfuscation would override
the evidence.

The bolt cutter used to open the lock to a box in
which a .22 caliber handgun was kept, a handgun
Louisa Cormier used to practice with; the manuscript with two bullet holes Louisa had taken from
the dead hands of Charles Lutnikov and which she
had frantically been copying; the evidence that
Lutnikov was writing Louisa Cormier's novels.

Aiden put on her coat and headed for the eleva-

tor, thinking, We still don't have the murder weapon
and we still don't have a motive and Louisa Cormier
has Noah Pease.

Maybe they should wait, keep gathering evidence, find the gun and a motive. But Mac had said
they had enough, and Aiden trusted his judgment.

"This is harassment," said Louisa Cormier when she
opened the door.

Aiden noticed that Louisa was holding her hands
together to try to keep them from shaking. Louisa's
eyes fell on the man in a blue suit with the two CSI
investigators.

"I'm not inviting you in," she said. "And I'm calling my attorney. I'll get an injunction against you
and the entire—"

"We don't want to come in," said Mac.

Louisa Cormier looked puzzled.

"You don't? Well I'm not, under advisement from
my attorney, answering any of your questions."

"You don't have to," said Mac. "But you do have
to come with us. You're under arrest."

"I . . ." Louisa began.

"And if you would, we'd like you to bring your
Walther with you. This detective will go with you to
get it. We do have the papers for that."

Mac reached into his jacket pocket and removed a
tri-folded sheet of paper.

"You can't," Louisa Cormier said. "I showed you
that gun. You know it hasn't been fired."

"We think it has," said Aiden.

Louisa Cormier began to collapse. Aiden stepped

forward to catch her and caught a whiff of the author's perfume, a gardenia scent exactly like the one Aiden's mother used.

Stevie worked his way slowly up the dark stairwell, dragging his reluctant leg behind him. When he hit the main-floor landing, the bakery smells came through the doors to his left.

Stevie liked the bakery, the smell of fresh bread, driving the truck, talking to the customers on his route. He knew it would all be gone in a few minutes, that he would, one way or another, be gone. It was unfair, but his mistake had been in forgetting that life was unfair and putting his trust and loyalty in the pocket of Dario Marco.

Before he reached the last two steps and stepped into the corridor, he stood in the shadows and looked both ways. No one stirred.

Dario Marco's office was only three doors down on the right. Stevie did his best to hurry and to be quiet. He had to settle for being quiet.

If Helen Grandfield was there when he opened the door, he would probably kill her. He could do it quickly, not give her time to react. She had been part of the set-up. Daughter of Dario Marco, niece of Anthony Marco, she had been part of what he knew now was a plan to make Stevie, Stupid Stevie, Loyal Stevie, the fall guy.

He paused at the door to the office and listened. He heard nothing. He opened the door ready to pounce on a startled or off-guard Helen Grandfield. But there was no one in the outer office.

Stevie wondered if Dario was out, possibly for the day. It wouldn't be like him to miss a day, but the last few days had been like no others.

Stevie went to the inner door, listened again, heard nothing and slowly opened it. The lights were dim and the blinds closed, but Stevie could see Dario Marco behind his desk.

Dario looked up. Stevie was not prepared for what he saw, a calm Dario Marco who said, "Stevie, we've been waiting for you."

Out of the corner stepped Jacob the Jockey and Helen Grandfield. The Jockey had a gun in his hand, and it was aimed at Stevie.

The table in front of Joelle Fineberg's desk was crowded. She had the lowest seniority, actually none at all, so Joelle had the smallest office.

She had opted for a very small desk, a small bookcase, and room enough for the table around which six people could fit with reasonable comfort. She used the table as a work space, clearing it off for meetings like this one by simply gathering papers and books, placing them in a black plastic container, and slipping the container behind her desk and out of sight.

"You don't even have enough for a grand jury," said Noah Pease, his hand on the shoulder of Louisa Cormier, who sat next to him and looked straight ahead.

"I think we do," said Fineberg, who sat across from them with Mac on one side of her and Aiden on the other.

A neat pile of papers and photographs sat on the table like a deck of oversized cards waiting to be cut for a hard game of poker, which was close to what they were playing.

Fineberg looked at Mac and said, "Detective, would you go over the evidence once more?"

Mac looked down at the yellow pad in front of him and went step-by-step over the evidence. Then she looked up at Aiden, who nodded her agreement.

Pease's face remained blank. So did Louisa Cormier's.

"Would it surprise you to know that Detectives Taylor and Burn found your client's fingerprints on seven different items in Charles Lutnikov's apartment?" said Fineberg.

"Yes," said Pease. "It would."

Fineberg went through the pile of papers in the stack and came up with seven photographs. She held them out to Pease.

"Perfect match," said the assistant DA. "A cup, a countertop, the desk, and four on bookshelves."

The fingerprints were a perfect match to Louisa Cormier's.

Louisa Cormier reached for the photographs.

"Circumstantial," said Pease with a sigh.

"Your client lied to us about ever being in Lutnikov's apartment," Fineberg said.

"I've been there once," said Louisa. "Now I remember. He asked me to pick up . . . something."

"You have a reason why we're here?" asked Pease.

"Negotiation," said Fineberg.

"No," said Pease, shaking his head.

"Then we go before the grand jury asking for Murder Two," said Fineberg.

She turned to Mac and said, "Detectives Taylor and Burn will testify. He's convinced by the evidence the CSI unit has gathered and so am I. A jury will be too."

"Ms. Cormier is a highly respected literary figure with no motive," said Pease. "Your case stands on the argument that she did not write her own books. She did."

"Detective Taylor?" said Fineberg.

"Convince me. Convince my expert," said Mac.

"How?" asked Pease.

"Have her write something," said Fineberg.

"Ridiculous," said Pease.

"She has four days before we go in front of the grand jury," said Fineberg. "Five pages. That shouldn't be impossible, especially when a murder charge is involved."

"I couldn't write under this pressure," said Louisa Cormier, handing the photographs of the fingerprints back to her lawyer, who placed them neatly on the table and slid them across to Fineberg.

"You're counting on a jury having sympathy for a famous and much-loved celebrity," said Fineberg. "How quickly we forget Martha Stewart. You could, of course, counter with O.J. Simpson, but . . ."

Pease was looking at Fineberg now with an irritation that might well have already turned to open hostility in a less-experienced lawyer.

"We get to that grand jury," said Fineberg, "and

our case comes out, at least enough of it to get a True Bill."

A True Bill, as both lawyers knew, is a written decision of the grand jury, signed by the jury foreperson, that it has heard sufficient evidence from the prosecution to believe that an accused person has probably committed a crime and should be indicted.

"And damage my client's reputation," said Pease. "As will any plea bargain."

"We have the gun," said Fineberg, looking at Mac.

"We're testing the gun in Ms. Cormier's drawer," he said.

"Which you've already determined has not been—" Pease began.

"It matches the bullet we found at the bottom of the elevator shaft," said Mac. "Ms. Cormier shot Charles Lutnikov, put on her coat, dropped her gun and the bolt cutter, which she'd probably had in her trophy case, into her tote bag, locked the elevator on her floor, and hurried down the stairs in time to take her usual, morning walk. It was eight on a snowy blizzard-like weekend. It wasn't likely anyone in her section of the building would be up and trying to get the elevator for hours. Besides, she planned to be gone only about thirty minutes."

"And where does your fanciful story assume my client went?" asked Pease.

"To Drietch's firing range, four blocks away," said Mac. "Even in the snow and ice she could make it in fifteen minutes. I just did by walking fast. She knew the range wasn't open for another three hours on a Saturday. She opened the outer door with a simple credit card. Her detective in three of her books has done the same thing. Ms. Cormier had probably checked that it could be done."

"Premeditation," said Joelle Fineberg.

"Your client went to the room where the guns are stored," Mac went on. "She cut the bolt on the box containing the gun she used at the range, took the gun out, dropped it in her purse and replaced it with the murder weapon. Then she threw the cut lock onto the firing range. She knew someone would eventually notice, after she switched the guns again, that the range Walther would be found, that any competent detective would know it hadn't been fired recently and she knew an examination of the gun and bullet would show they didn't match, but she didn't think it would come to that. If Drietch or anyone checked the box even before the switch was made again, they'd think they were seeing the gun that was normally kept there. Ms. Cormier was reasonably confident that they wouldn't check, but it really didn't matter."

"How far-fetched can—?" Pease said.

"I suggest you read one of your client's first three novels if you want to see how far-fetched a story she can come up with."

Pease shook his head wearily as if listening to Mac was an undeserved punishment he would have to endure.

Mac ignored the lawyer and went on.

"Ms. Cormier went back home quickly, put the bolt cutter in the basement, went up the stairs, released the elevator so it would go down to the first floor, and put the gun she had taken from the shooting range into her drawer."

"And then?" Pease asked, shaking his head as if he were being forced to listen to a fairy tale.

"She waited for us to come and readily showed us the gun, practically insisted on it. It was the gun she had taken from the range, not the one she always kept in her drawer. When we were gone, she went back to the range, said she wanted to practice and switched the guns again, leaving the one that was usually in the box. Officer Burn went to the range, examined the gun, and determined that it wasn't the murder weapon."

"Your client hid the murder weapon in plain sight," said Fineberg. "In the drawer of her desk. She did it thinking that CSI wouldn't examine it a second time after determining that it hadn't been fired."

"The bullet is going to match your gun," Mac said to Louisa Cormier. "You made the whole thing too complicated."

"It almost worked," whispered Louisa Cormier.

"Louisa," Pease warned, leaning over to whisper to his client before sitting up. "Self defense," he said. "Charles Lutnikov came to my client's apartment after threatening her on the phone. She had the gun out to protect herself. He tried to wrestle it from her. It went off. She panicked."

"And then thought out the elaborate cover-up on the spot," said Fineberg.

"Yes," said Pease. "She's a writer with a very active imagination."

"Who didn't write her own books," said Mac.

"We'll see what a jury thinks about that," said Pease.

"Why would Lutnikov threaten Ms. Cormier?"

Neither lawyer nor client spoke.

"Involuntary manslaughter," said Pease. "Suspended sentence."

"No," said Fineberg. "The evidence these officers have gathered shows intent, premeditation, and cover-up."

Pease leaned over to whisper in Louisa Cormier's ear. A look of horror came over her face.

"Murder Two," said Fineberg.

"Manslaughter," said Pease. "Nothing goes public. You pick a judge who will seal the record. Say what you like to the media."

Fineberg looked at Mac and then turned to Pease, shaking her head.

"Off the record?" Pease said, patting his client's hand.

"Off the record," said Fineberg.

"Louisa?" Pease said, hand on her arm ready to guide her with gentle pressure.

"I can't," Louisa Cormier said, looking at Pease.

Pease cocked his head and said, "They can't use it unless we let them."

Louisa Cormier sighed.

"I shot Charles Lutnikov. He was blackmailing me," she said, looking at the table, hands folded white-knuckled in front of her now.

"You had been paying him for writing your books," said Fineberg.

"It wasn't about money," Louisa said. "It was

about writing credit. He wanted all my future books to bear both of our names as author. I offered him more money. He wasn't interested."

"So you shot him?" asked Fineberg.

"He said he was bringing up the manuscript of the new book and that he would give it to me only if I had a notarized statement saying that the book would bear both of our names. I couldn't have that. People, editors, reviewers would start to think about my previous books, and Charles couldn't be counted on to keep from telling about his helping me with the previous books."

"And . . . ?" Fineberg said after a long pause by Louisa Cormier.

"When he came up, I stopped the elevator. The manuscript was in his hands, clutched to his chest like a baby. He wanted it to be our baby. I tried to reason with him, told him that if we continued the way we were I'd help him get his own books published. He wasn't interested. He reached over to the elevator buttons and pressed a button when it happened."

"You shot him," said Fineberg.

"I didn't mean to," she said. "I just wanted to threaten him, warn him, frighten him, have him hand me the manuscript. The elevator door closed on my hand. He grabbed for the gun. He was enraged. The gun fired. The doors opened again. I could see he was dead. I hit the button to stop the elevator and took the manuscript from him."

"Unfortunate accident. No. Self defense," said Pease with a broad smile.

"Then why hide the gun," Fineberg said. "Why make all of this up?"

"My career, my . . . I was frightened," Louisa Cormier said.

"You didn't plan to shoot him, but you immediately thought of a plan, a very complicated plan, as soon as you shot him. You were on your way to the firing range with the gun and a bolt cutter minutes, maybe seconds, after you shot Lutnikov," said Fineberg skeptically.

"Make an offer, Ms. Fineberg," Pease said. "Make it a good one."

17

"SORRY ABOUT THIS, STEVIE," said Dario Marco, seated behind his desk. "You're a good worker, a loyal employee, a good guy."

Stevie stood on a leg that threatened to give way and looked dumbly and open-mouthed at the man behind the desk who had been his boss, his protector.

"Problem here, you see," said Marco, sitting back and adjusting his jacket to get rid of the wrinkles, "is that we need to give the police someone. They've been all over the place. They've got evidence against you on the Spanio killing and you killed a cop and shot another one. Big problem is you killed the cop right outside the door you just came through. So, what can I do? I mean, I ask you?"

Stevie said nothing.

Marco shrugged to show again that he had no choice. "Besides which, you really are one dumb bastard and you're getting old."

Stevie looked at Jake, who had betrayed him, and then at Helen Grandfield who had no expression.

"Dad," Helen said. "Let's just do it."

"I owe Stevie an explanation," Dario said patiently.

"He came here to kill you," she said.

"That's so," Dario Marco agreed. "And he broke in, and it was fortunate that we had a gun."

"The Jockey doesn't have a permit," said Stevie, trying to think.

"That's right," said Marco. "He's a convicted felon. You're dumb, but not that dumb. The gun is mine. I've got a permit. Jacob picked it up from the desk where I had just finished cleaning it when you . . ."

"Why?" asked Stevie. "You set me up, right from the start. You wanted the cops to come for me. Why?"

"Back up," said Dario. "Believe me, I wanted you to get away. Why would I lie now? But in business you cover your ass. You're getting old, Stevie. You're going to slow down. Shit, you're already slowing down. Look at yourself. Now you've broken into my office and said you were going to kill me. In front of three witnesses."

Dario Marco nodded at Jacob, who looked at Stevie and hesitated.

"He set you up too, Jake," said Stevie.

"Shoot the old fart," said Marco.

The leap across the desk by Stevie was a surprise to everyone in the room, probably even Stevie. When his stomach hit the table, all feeling left his wounded leg. He reached out for Dario's neck and found it. He was doing what he was good at now, dumb or no dumb.

"Shoot," Helen shouted.

Jake fired and missed. His hand was shaking, but Stevie's weren't. Lying on his stomach on the desk, he lifted Dario from the chair and snapped his neck.

Helen was on his back now, clawing at his face, grunting, screaming. Jake looked for an open shot. Dario Marco's body slipped down, eyes open in surprise, chin resting on the edge of the desk. Stevie threw Helen Grandfield off of him. She tripped backwards, going over a chair.

Stevie tried to stand. He turned his head toward the Jockey, who had backed away trembling, two hands on the gun. No way Stevie could make the lunge before he was shot. He dug into his pocket and clutched the dog Lilly had given him.

"Stop," said a voice.

Jake over his gun, Helen over the overturned chair she had fallen behind, Stevie over his shoulder, saw the uniformed cop, the one who Stevie had bypassed at the front door on his way in. The cop had heard the shot.

The cop, whose name was Rodney Landry, was a bodybuilder with four years on the force. He knew what to do: aim his weapon at the tiny man next to the desk. From the description he had been given, Landry knew that the man with the bloody leg, who, for some inexplicable reason, was lying on the desk, was the one he had been told to look for.

From where he stood, Landry, weapon in hand, did not see Dario Marco.

"Put the weapon down on the floor very slowly," Landry ordered.

Jake wanted to hurry, but he forced himself to bend slowly and place the weapon on the floor. Stevie managed to turn his body and get up on one elbow.

"He broke in here," Helen Grandfield screamed, pointing at Stevie. "He killed my father."

Landry could see it now. It looked like a joke, a Halloween joke. The dead man's head seemed to be resting on his chin behind the desk. His eyes were wide open and he looked surprised, very surprised.

Stevie, feeling nothing in his leg now, reached into his pocket, clutched the painted dog, and smiled.

Ed Taxx made the deal. States evidence against Dario Marco and his daughter in exchange for Murder Two minimum. He talked it through and then wrote it out. He knew the drill, followed it. He also had enough money hidden away to take care of his family and he didn't want the police going into his life or looking through his bank accounts.

"I take down Dario Marco and Helen Grandfield with me and you drop any further investigation of me or my assets," said Taxx.

"And whatever you have on Anthony Marco," Ward said.

"I don't have much there," said Taxx.

"We'll take what you can give us," said Ward.

Taxx sat across the table from Assistant DA Ward and CSI Investigator Danny Messer, prepared to tell his story.

"So what do I get?" asked Taxx.

"Depends on your story," said Ward.

"It's a good one," said Taxx.

He had been approached by Helen Grandfield, who didn't tell him how she knew he had been assigned to the Alberta Spanio protection detail nor how she knew he had prostate cancer that had spread to his other organs. Taxx really didn't care how she knew. He hadn't told his wife or family about the cancer. He had some money put away but it would have drained whatever his family would have to live on just to make his final months stretch into a less painful year. Now the irony was that the state would have to pay for his treatment.

When he met with Dario Marco he had been offered one hundred and fifty thousand in cash to simply give Alberta Spanio an overdose of sleeping pills, and leave the bathroom window unlocked after screwing the hook into it.

"Why?" asked Ward.

"Helen Grandfield told me later that someone was supposed to be let down to the window from the room above, but the storm made it impossible. Then at three in the morning I was to have a coughing fit that lasted three minutes to cover the noise if there was any."

Taxx accepted, got the cash in advance.

"So far," he explained to Assistant DA Ward, with whom Taxx had worked for fifteen years, "no problem."

"And then?" asked Ward.

"Night it was supposed to happen I got a call," said Taxx. "Cell phone. Collier was in the room. I pretended it was my wife. It was Helen Grandfield. She told me what to do: break down Spanio's door in the morning, send Collier to check the bathroom because there was obviously a window open, get to the bed fast, and stab Spanio in the neck. No problem again. I was careful with my words, saying something like, 'No, honey, tell him it will have to be what we already have plus double.' Collier was watching a basketball game on television, but I knew he heard. Helen put her hand over the mouthpiece I think, checking with Dario, came back and said it was a deal. I don't think they ever planned to send anyone through the window. I think they counted on my killing Alberta from the beginning."

"And?"

"Spanio was out from the pills and the cold when we broke the door down. I stepped in between him and the bed so he couldn't see the body and nodded toward the bathroom. Collier went into the bathroom. I took the knife out of my pocket and stabbed Alberta in the neck. Four or five seconds at most. Collier came out of the bathroom. I had stepped back so he could see the knife in her neck. I watched him head into the other room to call for backup."

"And that's when you had a problem?" said Ward. Taxx nodded.

"I went into the bathroom. The window was open. "My first thought was, 'Great, Collier saw that. He thinks the perp came in through the window and went back out through the window.' That's when I realized the snow was piled up on the sill. No one could have gotten through the window without disturbing the snow."

"And that's when you made your mistake," said Ward.

Taxx nodded.

"I swept the snow out the window with my sleeve," he said. "Instead of inside into the tub. I could hear Collier on the phone in the front room. I came out of the bathroom before he could come back in, saying we had a crime scene and should wait in the other room for CSI. I didn't want him back in the bathroom seeing the snow gone."

"And?" Ward coaxed.

"Yesterday I went to a Chinese restaurant and met with Helen Grandfield," said Taxx. "Collier must have been suspicious. He followed me. I spotted him across the street. He could check with my wife and find out she hadn't called me the night before. He could look at the crime-scene photographs and notice that the snow had been cleared from the bathroom window."

"So, you told Helen Grandfield, who told you that she would take care of it," said Ward. "And she paid you the rest of the money."

"I have nothing to say about that," said Taxx.

"You knew they were going to kill Collier," said Ward.

Taxx didn't answer for a beat and then said, "I didn't want to think about that."

"Where's the money they paid you?"

Again, Taxx didn't answer. In addition to the money he had put away and what he had gotten from Dario Marco, he had a million dollar life insurance policy.

"I'll tell Stella," said Danny Messer.

Aiden opened the top drawer in Louisa Cormier's desk.

"It's not here," she said, looking up at Mac.

"Someone must have stolen it," said Louisa.

"You have a safe?" asked Mac.

Louisa turned to Pease, who sighed.

"Your client can open it or we can," said Mac. "My guess is that it's in this room, but we can . . ."

"Open it Louisa," said Pease. "Cooperate."

Louisa Cormier went to the bright-red painting of a flower by Georgia O'Keeffe and flipped it back. On the wall was the safe.

Louisa looked at Pease who nodded at her to open the safe. She shook her head "no" but he urged her on.

"We can deal with this," Pease said gently. "You acted in self defense."

Louisa opened the safe and with a gloved hand Aiden reached in and pulled out the .22 Walther. This time she felt certain she had a match for her bullet.

"You made a mistake my Pat Fantome would never have made," said Louisa.

"Louisa," Pease warned, but his client couldn't resist.

"You didn't check the serial number on the gun in my desk when you first came here," she said. "You would have found that it wasn't my gun, that it was

Mathew Drietch's, but you had no reason to check it. I came this close to succeeding."

Louisa held up her right hand showing a quarter of an inch of space between thumb and finger.

"Charles Lutnikov's Pat Fantome might have checked that serial number," Mac admitted. "But Pat Fantome isn't real. We are. We make mistakes and then we take care of those mistakes."

Mac read Louisa Cormier her Miranda rights.

The metal mesh door swung open and Anthony Marco in prison orange looked at Ward and Mac.

"No pretty woman this time?" Marco said.

"She's a little under the weather," said Mac.

"I'll send her flowers," said Marco with a smile.

"What's this about?" asked Marco's lawyer.

"Trials moving fast," said Marco. "We've got a deal."

"No, we don't," said Ward. "We don't need your cooperation."

Anthony Marco looked over his shoulder at his lawyer and then back at Mac and Ward.

"What?" asked Marco.

"You know a Steven Guista?"

"No," said Anthony, sitting up straight.

"He knows you," said Ward. "He knows a lot about you and your brother and he's been added to the witness list. He'll be testifying."

"Against me?" asked Anthony, pointing to himself.

Mac nodded.

"Word has it he murdered a cop and kicked the shit out of another one," said Anthony.

"I thought you didn't know him," said Ward.

"I lied."

"Guista's testimony won't stand," said Anthony's lawyer. "What did you offer him to commit perjury?"

"Nothing," said Ward. "He didn't ask for anything. We didn't offer him anything. You go right ahead and ask him when he's on the stand."

"I had nothing to do with having that Spanio woman killed," Anthony insisted. "That was Dario's idea."

"Your brother is dead," said Mac.

"No," Anthony protested.

"Have your lawyer make a call," said Mac.

"Dario's dead? The stupid son-of-a-bitch died and left me with . . . Can they do this? Can they do this to me?" Anthony asked his lawyer.

The attorney didn't answer.

Epilogue

THE SNOW HAD LET UP, but not the bitter cold. Mac stood, hands in his pockets, feet apart to keep the wind from pushing him away from Claire's gravesite. The tops of headstones peeked out of snow and Mac remembered that there had been some graves with simple brass markers, now buried two feet under snow.

The snowplow had come through carefully, and Mr. Greenberg, who had arranged for the clearing of the site, had shown up and supervised, pointing out where the plow should go and how a path through the snow from the parking circle should be opened.

Mac stood with the flowers in his hands, feeling the wind pulling at the bouquet of various colored roses—red, pink, white, yellow—which had been hard to get in the aftermath of the storm.

A thin wind whistled mournful music across the chill, peaceful silence of the morning. Greenberg, a thin little man who was at least sixty, with pink cheeks and a huge overcoat, stood discreetly back, hands folded in front of him. Mac took a few steps toward the grave.

Behind him he heard the sound of a vehicle coming down from the cemetery gates to the turnaround where Mac had parked.

He didn't turn. He was now right next to the headstone, reading the etched words in the stone. He heard footsteps on the path, and now he did turn around. Don Flack, Aiden, Stella, and Danny were moving toward him. Stella leaned a little on Danny's arm.

"You shouldn't be out of the hospital," Mac said as they approached.

"It's your anniversary," Stella answered. "Wouldn't want to miss that."

They gathered around the grave and Mac knelt to place the flowers on it against the stone to give them a little protection from the wind.

Greenberg moved in quickly and secured the flowers with a smooth rounded rock. Then he stood up and handed each person there a small stone.

"If you like," said Greenberg. "It's a tradition. We place a stone of remembrance each year by the grave of a loved one."

Mac looked at the small brown stone in his hand and placed it atop the granite tombstone. Stella, Aiden, Danny, and Flack followed. Then all except Mac stepped back.

There was nothing to say. There was nothing he needed to say. He stood for what seemed like a long time before turning and joining the others in the walk back down the path.